She might as well discover what kissing was about while she had the chance.

Miss Partland had been smacked on the lips by Squire's son one afternoon after his lessons with her father. But this was nothing at all like that. There was nothing furtive or frenzied in the viscount's kiss; it simply felt nice, all tingly, with snowflakes on his lips. Very nice, very nonthreatening because Kathlyn knew he wasn't going to maul her or ask for more than she was willing to give. Exceptionally nice. By the time his lordship was done with the pretend kiss, the just-for-show kiss, Kathlyn's knees were like jelly, and she couldn't feel her toes at all. . . .

SNOWDROPS
AND
SCANDALBROTH

Barbara Metzger

FAWCETT CREST • NEW YORK

A Fawcett Crest Book
Published by Ballantine Books
Copyright © 1997 by Barbara Metzger

All rights reserved under International and Pan-American Copyright Conventions. Published in the United States by Ballantine Books, a division of Random House, Inc., New York, and simultaneously in Canada by Random House of Canada Limited, Toronto.

http://www.randomhouse.com

Library of Congress Catalog Card Number: 96-97063

ISBN 0-449-22506-2

Manufactured in the United States of America

First Edition: February 1997

10 9 8 7 6 5 4 3 2 1

For Miles Quinn Todaro
Welcome

Chapter One

Snow, damn it!

"Blast! I knew we shouldn't have driven so far afield today," said Courtney Choate, Viscount Chase, frowning at the white stuff swirling around his precious matched bays. "At least we should have taken the heavier traveling carriage and team."

"Oh, pooh, then we would have needed the driver and the groom, and I would have had to bring my maid along with us in the closed coach. We wouldn't have any time to be alone, Courtney, only the two of us." The sweet suggestion in Miss Adelina Marlowe's voice should have melted his annoyance, if not the snow, but Lord Chase's brow stayed furrowed. He'd driven his valuable cattle miles over rutted country roads just to spend an interminable hour making small talk and balancing a teacup on his knee.

"I don't think your parents meant for us to be alone in a curricle, more than two hours from your house, during a blizzard."

"Fiddle, it's merely a flurry. Besides, we had to visit Sukey Fanshawe today. She and her sisters are all leaving for Bath tomorrow, remember?" Adelina scooted her rounded posterior along the cushioned bench until her softness was pressed against his thigh, which would have warmed his blood if not for his greatcoat and her fur-lined pelisse and the freezing wind that was doing its best to play chaperone. "And I had to show off my new fiancé, didn't I?"

It was a measure of man's vanity that Courtney forgot about the snow, forgot about his horses, forgot that his better judgment had been overridden. This Diamond, this Toast, this perfect embodiment of young English womanhood, was his—right down to the droplet of moisture on the end of her aristocratic nose. And she was pleased enough with her bargain that she wanted to gloat over him!

Courtney knew he was a prize on the matrimonial market—a nobleman with reputation, fortune, and teeth all still intact couldn't be anything else—but the beautiful Miss Marlowe had been turning down eligible *partis* for the three years since her come-out. Courtney never dreamed for a moment that she'd toss her bonnet at him. As a matter of fact, he never dreamed of getting leg-shackled so young. He was just twenty-three, after all, and the only contemporaries of his who were married were those who'd needed to mend their purses with their wives' portions. Courtney Choate, Lord Chase, had no such need.

He did have other needs, though, which Miss Adelina Marlowe would satisfy delightfully with her silky, enthusiastic femininity. Yes, he'd come to agree with his grandfather that marriage was a fine idea. He also had come to agree with His Grace, the Duke of Caswell, that Adelina was a fine choice. A baron's daughter, she brought a handsome dowry, excellent connections, and a familiarity with the polite world that a younger female wouldn't have. Any of the simpering debs Lord Chase knew would be all atwitter right now. They'd be complaining of the cold, worrying about their complexions in the breeze, panicking at the thought of being overturned into a snowbank. Sukey Fanshawe with her high-pitched giggles and fluttering eyelashes would be in tears. Not his Adelina. She merely tucked a wayward gold curl back under her hood, then tucked her little gloved hand into the crook of his arm. He smiled down at her, trying to ignore that drip on her nose.

Unfortunately, his lordship's lack of concentration permitted his outside horse, Castor, to shy at the wind-driven snow, which caused the inside horse, Pollux, to lose his gait, which rocked the carriage from side to side until Courtney had them back under control. Miss Marlowe was smiling gamely, but Pollux was limping.

"Blast!" Lord Chase got down and inspected the animal's leg. "He'll have to be walked," the viscount reported when he regained the driver's bench. "Confound it, I knew we should have taken your father's carriage."

"Oh, but Sukey's beau only drives a gig."

He ignored that, too.

What he couldn't ignore was the snow, falling even faster and heavier, obscuring the uneven roadbed and making the horses' steps more difficult and more dangerous. "I'll have to lead them."

After an hour, Courtney knew they were lost. They should have reached the crossroad to Marlowe Manor twenty minutes ago. Whatever lightness the day held was quickly fading, and there was nothing to be seen except snow. And more snow. Courtney walked back to the curricle.

" 'Twould be idiocy to continue in the dark. Lud knows your father will have my hide and your mother will have hysterics, but we'll have to find shelter for the night."

"La, they won't worry. They won't even know. Papa will assume we decided to stay on at Sukey's."

"But Sukey will know, and her sisters. Your reputation will be in tatters, my dear."

Adelina just shrugged, sending a small avalanche of snow off her shoulders and down onto his, at the curricle's

3

side. "The Fanshawes will all be in Bath, silly, and besides, we're engaged. No one cares about a betrothed female's reputation."

His grandfather cared. "I suppose we could move the wedding date forward if there is any talk."

"Now that would send Mama into spasms for certain. You must know she's reserved St. George's in Hanover Square for the first week in June. And my dress couldn't possibly be ready, nor all the invitations changed. Why, who would come to a wedding in the middle of the winter?"

While Miss Marlowe was going on about flowers and bridal attendants, Courtney was following a trail of cow droppings. Where there were cows, there might be a barn, a farmstead, a farmwife to play propriety and provide a hot meal.

"Did you say 'cowslip'? Mama thought roses, but I have a partiality for orchids. . . ."

By the time Courtney and the horses trudged through the snowdrifts to the barn, night had fallen. He couldn't see lights from the farm or a path, if there was one nearby. But the barn had a good roof and the cows provided warmth, and there was hay and grain for his horses. By the light of the coach lantern, Courtney mounded some straw into a bed for Adelina and covered it with the carriage blanket. "I'm sorry, Addie, but this is the best we can do."

She sniffed. "Adelina, if you please." Her smile returned when he proffered the silver flask from his greatcoat pocket. "Oh, brandy, how exciting! Don't you think this is the most romantic thing ever? We're warm and dry, and we're together. Of course, my poor toes are still numb. Do you think you could . . . ?"

He was the one who'd been slogging through the snow, but Courtney wasn't about to refuse a damsel in distress, so he knelt by her side in the straw and pulled off her only slightly dampened boots. Then he massaged her feet in their silk stockings.

4

"Oh, that feels good, but I'm still cold."

So he lay beside her and rubbed her back. What happened next was inevitable. It might have been inscribed on the very first snowflake of the afternoon, so predictable and preordained was the outcome. Not that Courtney meant to be anything less than a gentleman, of course. He intended to kiss Adelina good night, cover her with more straw, blow out the lantern, then make a nest for himself nearby with his greatcoat for cover. His good intentions lasted about as long as the lantern light. As the temperature and the level of the brandy fell, so did inhibitions.

The good-night kiss turned into several, each deeper and longer and more intense than the one that went before. Hands began to wander, searching for buttons and tapes and bare skin. Lord Chase and Miss Marlowe forgot the cold and the meager tea they'd partaken of hours ago. They forgot the hard ground, the barnyard smells, the rustling of creatures in the loft. They almost forgot they weren't married yet. Almost.

"Lud, we better stop while we can."

"Not yet, darling. Not yet. Who's to know?"

"I will."

"But no one expects the same restraints in engaged couples, remember? And isn't this better than freezing to death apart? Doesn't this feel good? And this?"

Good? Heaven should feel so good. Still, "It isn't right, my dear. We've waited this long. We can wait for our wedding night."

"I'm so tired of waiting. Aren't you?"

"Yes, but—"

"You want me, don't you? I can tell by how hard you're breathing that you do."

"Of course I do, but I can wait."

"Till June?" was the tortured reply. "If you loved me, you'd prove it to me tonight."

"Please, my dear, we have to be strong."

5

"But why? It's not such a big thing. I mean, it's not as if it's the first time or anything."

"Bloody hell." Courtney jumped up, dumping Adelina over onto the bare dirt floor. "It is for me!"

She peered up at him in the barn's gloom, her mouth hanging open. "You mean you're a virgin?"

"You mean you're not?"

What could she answer now? "But . . . but what about that house you keep in Kensington?"

He had turned his back, to straighten his clothes. He faced her again. "What do you know about my house in Kensington?"

"Everyone knows you visit there. Mama says every gentleman has outside interests that it's a wife's duty to ignore."

"Your mama was right, you should have ignored the gossip. Who I see in Kensington is none of your affair." He paused in lighting the lantern. "My God, exactly how many affairs have you had?"

"Simply because you're as pure as the driven snow doesn't make me a fallen woman, Mr. Holier-than-thou. There have been only three, if you must know, and the footman wasn't my fault. I was only fifteen and thought we were merely experimenting."

" 'Experimenting'? By Jupiter, what would you do in a chemistry laboratory? What of the others?" He had to know, even if it killed him.

"Well, you shouldn't hold the dancing master against me either, for he was French, don't you know. And then there was Peter Fanshawe, Sukey's brother, but I was going to marry him. I decided not to when you started paying your addresses. He's only a squire's son."

Courtney wasn't pulling his hair out, he was removing straw, but Adelina couldn't see that in the dark. She hurried on: "It's not as though I mean to play you false after we're married or anything. I do know all about providing a rightful heir and all that."

"And after? After you bless me with this legitimate token of your affection, what then?"

"Why, then we'd be free to go our own ways, like everyone else in the ton."

"You mean have affairs, slip in and out of bedrooms at house parties, have our names in the *on dits* columns? Not quite everyone wants that kind of marriage, Miss Marlowe. I don't. I heard my mother's cries too often to put another woman through that hell of infidelity, and I expect the same in my wife. I would not betray the woman I marry after taking our vows; I haven't betrayed her before either."

He might have said he was a Turkish pasha come to gather a harem. Adelina would have found it easier to comprehend. "But . . . but how? Why?"

How was easy: cold baths and pure thoughts and keeping one's pants buttoned. The why was harder to explain. His mother's experience was bad enough, common though it was, but his nursemaid had been abandoned by her husband for a redheaded actress, leaving her penniless and pregnant. Young Master Choate learned all about loyalty and faithfulness, if not with his mother's milk, then with his wet nurse's. A sickly child, he spent most of his time with these women, hearing enough about men's wickedness to give the devil's conscience a pang or two. Ideals forged in such iron are not easily bent. Courtney hadn't bent them yet; he wasn't going to now. He strode to the barn door to look out. When he came back he said, "I believe in the sanctity of marriage. That's what the Church teaches, that's what all the sermons preach. And if a woman's virtue is so highly acclaimed, a man's should be nothing less."

"This isn't the Middle Ages, Courtney, with those pure and perfect knights who wrote ballads and worshiped their ladies from afar. Those paragons only existed in fairy tales, you gudgeon. Real men have appetites, desires."

"They can also have morals and self-discipline. That's

7

what I've required of myself, that's what I require in a bride. I'm sorry, Miss Marlowe, but I cannot marry you."

"You what? You're crying off?" She beat her heels on the ground. "You can't do that! I'll be ruined."

"Why? You said yourself no one will know we spent the night alone. And it's not as if I'm leaving you in any different condition than I found you."

"But . . . but a gentleman never jilts a lady!"

Courtney was gathering up their belongings. "I don't think you're in any position to talk about correct behavior."

So she pulled her skirts down and her bodice up. "But I will, you dastard, I will talk. I'll tell everyone you're . . . you're . . ."

"A virgin?" he completed for her. "But who would believe you? And what kind of female speaks of such things? You would be damning yourself in the eyes of society, and if you stooped to blackmail, well . . . But you don't have to worry, I'll let you insert the notice ending the betrothal." He started to lead the horses out of their stalls. "The snow has stopped and the moon is out. We can be on our way."

Adelina crossed her arms over her chest. "Papa will never let you toss me over like this. The settlements, don't you know."

"They haven't been signed. But let me tell you, if by some chance you do manage to hold me to this engagement just so you can call yourself Lady Chase, you'll find yourself married and shipped off to my property in Cornwall before the cat can lick its ear. I doubt there's even a lighthouse keeper there you'd wish to seduce. No trips to London, no balls or fancy gowns, no chance of betraying me or disgracing my family name."

No presiding over the ton? She'd rather marry Peter Fanshawe then. Adelina reached for her boots. She also reached for what is more commonly found on barn floors. She waited, then threw a handful of manure at Courtney when he walked past her.

"I take it you now agree that we wouldn't suit." He wiped his cheek, then handed her his handkerchief to wipe her hands. "Oh, and do blow your nose."

Chapter Two

$\mathcal{I}$t wasn't snowing in Lord Marlowe's study, but the temperature had dropped by ten degrees in the last ten seconds. Courtney thought he might never feel his toes again, after that frigid walk back. Then again, he might never leave this room alive. Lord Marlowe's pouchy cheeks were reaching the purple stage, and his plump fingers were reaching for his dueling pistol. They came up with a penknife instead, to Courtney's relief, and the baron began butchering an innocent quill. The viscount watched slivers fly as he edged closer to the fireplace, letting his host and erstwhile prospective father-in-law rage on.

"What do you mean, you've both decided you won't suit? You suit to a cow's thumb, by George! You're both wellborn to titled families. My gal's no great heiress, but her portion is respectable enough that you can't say this was cream-pot convenience. You make a handsome couple, and I expected handsome grand-children, b'gad! The two of you are of similar ages, educated to your stations, and know all of the same people."

Not quite all, Courtney thought, trying to warm his hands by the meager fire. He didn't know that footman, for one, or the dancing master. His sense of honor couldn't let him besmirch a lady's name, of course, so he merely apologized again for declaring himself before he and Miss Marlowe had time to become well enough acquainted.

"Time? What's time got to do with it, sirrah? Lady Marlowe and I met in church the day we were wed. Arranged marriage, don't you know, and all for the best. Three sons, and the prettiest chit in the county. Aye, that's what I should have done, made a match for her myself, instead of listening to this true-love tripe."

"I'm sure Miss Marlowe will be happiest with the man of her choice."

"Balderdash! She chose you, didn't she? Mealy-mouthed gudgeon who lets a featherheaded chit change her mind after the notices've been sent. And cow-handed to boot. Demmit, you're not the man your grandfather promised."

Marlowe's daughter wasn't the lady he promised either. And a cow-handed driver? Hell, Courtney would guide his pair through the snow-covered Alps rather than stay one more night under this roof.

Courtney's conversation with his grandfather was slightly more heated, both the ducal drawing room and the duke's temper. Lord Marlowe had already canceled their weekly chess game, and His Grace was only slightly less aggravated at the loss of the granddaughter-in-law he'd approved.

"What the deuce did you do to the chit to make her cry off, anyway, you jackanapes?" he shouted, thumping his cane on the floor, and not for the first time, judging by the bare spot in the carpet. Viscount Chase took a practiced step backward, out of range. "Didn't take you for a flat who'd rush his fences with a gently bred girl, by all that's holy. Oh well, that female has her sights set on the strawberry leaves and tiara. You'll be able to talk her 'round."

11

Courtney said, "I have no intentions of pursuing the matter," then ducked.

The cane went flying as he knew it would. "What, a broken engagement? Never. I forbid you to bring such disgrace on the family, boy. That's bad ton."

"Better bad ton than a bad marriage. I'm sorry, Your Grace, but I cannot wed Miss Marlowe."

A book followed the cane. "Then you better find some other chit willing to put up with your fits and starts, and you better do it before careful fathers start keeping their daughters out of your clutches. I want an heir, do you hear me? I could pop off any day, and where would that leave the dukedom? In the hands of some rattlepate who could break his neck tomorrow in a steeplechase race, like your clunch of a father. I won't have it, I tell you! Now get out and don't come back till you've found another mother for my heir."

Lord Chase got out, muttering how if the duke wanted another heir so badly, His Grace might as well wed and bed Miss Marlowe himself. Everyone else seemed to have.

His mama, writing from Trowbridge, outside of Bath, blamed Miss Marlowe, of course. The female must be dicked in the nob, Rosemary, Lady Chase, wrote, to toss aside a prize catch like her dearest Courtney. Perhaps that's why Adelina was still on the shelf after three Seasons. He was better out of the match if such instability ran in the Marlowe family. And that's what she was telling all her friends when they shook their heads and clucked their tongues over the broken betrothal. Lady Chase only hoped his heart wasn't broken. She'd help him find a more perfect wife, come spring.

The only sensible response to the viscount's ended engagement came, as usual, from Nanny Dawson, when he visited her at that house in Kensington. His retired nursemaid merely shrugged over her sewing and said, "If it wasn't right, it wasn't right, and you'll know it when it is. Meantime, don't listen to the gossip. You know it'll all blow away like last week's snow. Come the snowdrops, those nodcocks will have something better to talk about."

Unfortunately the gossip didn't die, nor did the gabble-grinders find a choicer tidbit, for a woman scorned had a hellish score to settle. Adelina couldn't keep her mouth closed any more than she could her legs.

The baron's daughter wasn't precisely shunned on her return to London for the Season; no one gave her the cut direct or pulled their skirts aside when she passed. Her vouchers to Almack's weren't even rescinded. On the other hand, neither was she welcomed by her usual throngs of admirers or avalanches of invitations. Adelina Marlowe was firmly labeled a jilt, a flirt, a fussy female, none of them good recommendations for a bride. She was twenty-one, going on imminent and eternal spinsterhood. If she didn't find a husband this Season, she might as well put on caps. And Peter Fanshawe had gone off to India.

What was a girl to do? Adelina defended her honor in the usual way of a woman without any of that precious commodity: with innuendo. She couldn't admit that Viscount Chase had found her wanting, of course, so she insinuated, implied, and indicated, to her intimates only, that he was somewhat wanting as a man. Suddenly the talk was not about Miss Marlowe's next conquest, but about who—or what—his lordship visited at that place in Kensington.

"I always did think Chase was too pretty by half," went one conversation at White's. "Blond curls and blue eyes like a cherub. Fellow even has dimples, so m'sister says."

"But he's a bruising rider, just like his father."

"Chap was raised by his mother, though, don't you know."

At Almack's one of the gilt-chair brigade sighed. "He's such an excellent dresser."

"Too excellent, perhaps," her companion replied.

Another sigh. "But look at how he fills his inexpressibles."

"Sawdust and socks, my dear, sawdust and socks."

Courtney knew he was a topic of speculation; he simply didn't know why. He was receiving sidelong glances, stifled giggles, and even a pinch in the crowded corridor at Drury Lane. Then he received a furious letter from his grandfather, threatening to disown him for bringing shame to the family, and a tearstained one from his mother, who suddenly changed her mind about returning to London for the Season.

His valet quit. "I have my own reputation to consider, milord."

"What, is mine so bad, because I'm not going to make a match with some spoiled Toast?"

"No, it's fear that you might make a match with some spoiled, ah, milquetoast."

Viscount Chase tossed the man out on his disloyal, distrustful, disgusting ear. And bought himself a half-tamed stallion to ride in the park. And wore his clothes slightly mussed, which was easy since he didn't hire another valet. And spent twice as many hours as usual at Jackson's Boxing Parlour and Antoine's Fencing Academy. No matter, he found himself alone in the changing rooms.

Invitations to social events still arrived by the dozens. Of course they did, he was still a wealthy, unwed peer. Invitations to mills and card games and shooting matches, though, dwindled to a handful. Even his best friends Algie and Woody had taken themselves off to Newmarket for the training races. Thunderation, what the devil of a coil!

Dash it, was he the only untried young man in all of England not in religious orders? Were ape-leaders, unfledged debs, and Courtney Choate the last virgins on earth? Heaven knew staying chaste wasn't easy. It was deuced hard, in fact. Often. Hell, if it weren't hard, *then* it would be easy.

In his schoolboy days, Courtney was barely tempted to stray from his standards. The females available to him then were a blowzy, sordid lot, selling their favors and the French pox indiscriminately. London, though, was rife with temptation, especially for a man with money. Actresses, ballet dancers, and gambling hall dealers tumbled into a rich man's lap regularly. Professional birds of paradise preened themselves along the horse paths in the park. Or else, if a gentleman balked at paying for his pleasure, a bauble or a bouquet brought him the bedroom keys to the willing widows and the straying spouses of the beau monde. A man wasn't simply encouraged to partake of the buffet of unsanctified sex; he was expected to. And oh, how hungry Courtney was to sample the delicacies.

He wasn't a monk. He admired women, respected women, loved women. He loved their infinite differences, their universal softness, their curves and shadows and hidden secrets. But he had principles. Now he had a problem.

The way he saw it, through the bottom of a bottle of brandy, he had two choices. First, he could sacrifice his ethics to save his reputation. That is, he could fornicate his way back into favor. Having come this far with his beliefs and his personal honor unshaken, though, Courtney wasn't ready to concede. Stubborn pride wouldn't let him give up now, not when he knew he was right. There *was* a place for virtue in the world, even if he was the only unmarried man who practiced it.

There was another option. He could prove his masculinity by joining the army and dying a hero. A rake or a redcoat, those were his hellish choices, to become a womanizer or cannon fodder. The former would devastate his mother; the latter would give his grandfather apoplexy. Courtney chose the army.

Lieutenant Choate distinguished himself on the battlefield. He had to outride, outshoot, outbrave the bravest to prove his worth, and he did. Off the battlefield, he distinguished himself as being one of the few young officers not afflicted with parasites and personal ailments from visiting the camp followers. General Wellesley himself commended Courtney's valor and good sense. Frequently mentioned in the dispatches, the viscount won medals, promotions, and the admiration of his men—but nary an offer to share his tent with a fellow officer.

He did turn down other offers, from women with nothing to sell but their bodies. He gave them coins, food, or blankets when he could, but wasn't even tempted to take advantage of their misery. The occasional señorita he met at private parties for the general's staff, however, offered more enticement, especially when he thought of dying without ever really knowing a woman. Such morbid thoughts usually came during battles, though, when the now Captain Choate was too busy to change his uniform, much less his moral tenets. Instead, he did his damnedest to stay alive.

His body and his beliefs intact, Viscount Chase survived almost two years of the Peninsula campaign. In truth, he came closer to succumbing to a grandee's daughter than to a Frenchman's bullet.

One did eventually find its mark—a bullet, not a black-eyed beauty. Courtney was going home. His face was scarred, his thigh was shattered, his beliefs were bent but not broken, and he was a hero.

Everyone welcomed him, everyone accepted him, and everyone excused his peculiarities as a result of his war wounds. He wouldn't visit the new bordello? Of course not, his injury must be bothering him. The green room?

Too many stairs. Dinner at Harriet Wilson's? Too much exertion for his poor leg. Besides, he had someone waiting for him after the parties and card games and clubs, someone who would heat towels for his thigh and rub in liniment. Someone in Kensington.

"Of course you do, Court." Vernon Woodbury, known as Woody to his friends, was standing by Courtney's curricle outside White's that afternoon, ready to assist his ascent. "And we can all see how improved you are under her tender care. Ain't that right, Algie?"

Lord Algernon Lowe handed up the viscount's cane. "A hundred percent since you came home last month, old man. Why, I'd wager you'll be dancing a jig any day now. So when do we get to meet your ministering angel?"

"Meet her?"

"Can't keep her to yourself forever, Court." The expression on Woody's pale, babyish face was hopeful, almost beseeching his friend not to disappoint them again.

Algie gave him some breathing room. "Why don't you bring her to the Cyprians' Ball next month? You'll be stronger by then, even if you can't waltz. And should your ladybird be shy, well, she can wear a mask."

What Algie was saying was that, if the reason Courtney hadn't brought the female around was that he was ashamed of her looks, here was an opportunity to put the gossip to rest once and for all.

"I'll, ah, have to ask the lady," Courtney said, clucking to his horses to start before his friends could ask any more questions.

Damn and blast, Courtney thought as he drove through streets crowded with people going home to supper, now he'd have to go hire himself a mistress. A beautiful mistress, too, to hang on his arm at the Argyle Rooms. But that breed was almost as gossipy as their pedigreed sisters. If he failed to perform after paying for the services, his reputation would be back in the mud. If he did give up his fool's-gold goals and actually do the deed, he was liable to perform shabbily, from inexperience and lack of enthusiasm. Then he'd just be a laughingstock. Botheration. Besides, his leg was aching and it was snowing. Again.

Chapter Three

$\mathcal{I}$t was snowing again, oh dear. Kathlyn Partland was already two days late for her new governess position. Now she was lost in London, in the dark, in the snow. Oh dear indeed.

The hackney drivers must have taken their horses home to get out of the weather, Kathlyn thought, for there were no carriages to be hired. Therefore, if she did not wish to get to Lady Rotterdean's house in Berkeley Square three days late, she'd have to walk, which didn't faze her, country girl that she was. The garbled directions from a harassed stableboy did, though, and the unintelligible accents of the linkboys and crossing sweeps. Well, she was bound to come upon a major thoroughfare sooner or later, or someone who spoke the King's English. Kathlyn shifted her portmanteau to her other hand, pulled the hood of her mantle tighter, and plodded on.

Lady Rotterdean was sure to understand that none of the delay was Kathlyn's fault. She had to, for Kathlyn needed this position. She couldn't go back home, since there was no home back in Cheshire, even if her meager resources could have financed the return journey. The lease on the cottage was expired, not that Kathlyn could have paid the rent after her father died, even if his tiny annuity hadn't ended. They'd barely managed to make expenses when Papa was earning money tutoring. Mama's family had been no help, which was no surprise, either. They hadn't helped when Mama needed doctoring, and they hadn't helped when she needed burying. Kathlyn had written to her wealthy maternal aunt anyway. She was still waiting for a reply, three months after Papa went to his final reward. Heavens, the mails weren't that slow. Her own mail coach to London was only two days late, not three months, and that due to blizzards and bandits and Bow Street. Her aunt's delay was entirely attributable to meanness and miserliness. Kathlyn thanked goodness for the vicar's wife, who had a sister who sewed altar cloths with a neighbor of Lady Rotterdean, who needed a proper, educated female to be governess to her three daughters.

Kathlyn Partland was certainly educated, from sitting at so many of her father's lessons. Transcribing his notes perfected her penmanship, and juggling the household expenses taught her mathematics. As Papa's eyesight worsened, Kathlyn read to him for hours, history, geography, Latin, and Greek. She was more than qualified to teach three little girls—if she could only find them.

Kathlyn shifted the valise again. Her clothes and books must be picking up moisture from the snow, for the bag was growing heavier by the minute. Drat the snow, and drat the delay that meant Lady Rotterdean's coachman wasn't waiting for Kathlyn at the Swan Inn.

A tiny seed of resentment grew with the blister on Kathlyn's palm from the suitcase's straps. She had sent a note to Lady Rotterdean along with the driver's message to his dispatcher, explaining the problems and estimating their arrival. The man in the coaching office swore her note had been delivered. He'd also sworn Berkeley Square was a mere few blocks away. He wasn't the one toting a ton of baggage in wet shoes, in bone-chilling weather. Neither was Lady Rotterdean.

Kathlyn knew that she shouldn't have come. She

should have taken the vicar's offer to stay with him and his family until she found a position close to home. She shouldn't have let pride and determination send her haring off into the unknown, rather than accept charity. But the humble vicarage already held four children. Kathlyn had to make her own way in life, so she had to come to London. She simply should have planned better. But how could she have guessed the whole journey would be such a disaster?

First came the roadblock. The Royal Mail was just two changes out of Manchester, where Kathlyn had gotten on, when the carriage suddenly halted, amid much shouting and jingling of harness.

"It's highwaymen!" shrieked one of Kathlyn's fellow passengers. Mr. and Mrs. Tibbett were newlyweds visiting since Christmas with his family in Liverpool. A month with the in-laws was showing in the pale woman's frayed nerves. Mr. Tibbett patted her hand and chewed on his lip.

"Nonsense. It's broad daylight and this is His Majesty's Mail. No one would dare hold us up." Still, Mr. Lundquist, a wool merchant who plied his trade between York and London, removed his wallet from his coat pocket and stuffed it between the seat cushions.

Kathlyn lowered the window to see what was going on. Mrs. Tibbett screamed louder, as though the window were any protection from highwaymen. "There are two carts blocking the way," Kathlyn reported, "and some men are arguing with our driver." When Mrs. Tibbett's cries turned to muffled sobs, Kathlyn could make out the driver's angry words.

"No ha'penny shire sheriff can stop the Royal Mail, and Oi don't care how many bloody writs ye wave in me face. Now, get yer blasted turnip wagons off the road. Ye're costin' me time."

The local men stood their ground. "I got me orders from the magistrate," their leader yelled up at the coachman on his box. "I'm s'posed to search every carriage an' every wagon, lookin' for a dangerous criminal what broke out of gaol. You're obstructin' justice, that's what you're doin'. An' your guard is threatenin' a minion of the law with that there blunderbuss."

"Yer hayseed minion's goin' to be missin' an arm iffen you don't move those carts."

Kathlyn shook her head, opened the carriage door, and got out, despite Mrs. Tibbett's pleas. "This is absurd," she told the men on the ground waving pitchforks. "There is no escaped felon on board. And you," she added, addressing the box, "could have had us on our way ages ago if you'd only let them look." She held the door open and gestured for the leader of the posse to come see for himself.

The man bobbed his head and shuffled toward the carriage, one eye on the rifle in the guard's hands. He could see right off that there was no desperate outlaw in the coach, but he made a point of holding a poster up to poor Mr. Tibbett, whose wife was clinging like a limpet to his neck, throwing dagger looks at Kathlyn for subjecting them to such horrid indignity. "No, too young."

Mr. Lundquist, in his expensive, fur-collared overcoat, was too old. " 'Sides, he's sportin' a mustache. Our man's clean-shaved. You can cut it off, but you can't grow it back. Lessen you glue one on, I s'pose."

"Yes, yes, but Mr. Lundquist wouldn't do that. And you said yourself, he's too old." Which earned Kathlyn a scowl from that gentleman, but did end the scrutiny of the last of the rustic lawmen.

Outside of Stafford, the coach was halted again. This time Mrs. Tibbett was right to get distraught. The two masked men who rode out of the woods, firing their pistols and wounding the guard, really were highwaymen. Mr. Lundquist hid his wallet again. Amazingly, the bridle culls didn't demand money and jewels, which was a relief to Kathlyn, since she had precious little of the first and only her mama's locket of the second. Contrary to Mrs. Tibbett's high-pitched prediction, the high toby men weren't interested in rape or abduction either. They, too, wanted merely to search the carriage.

Whatever they were seeking wasn't there. The shorter of the men spit at the slamming door. "T'bastid couldn't a got far, not with me good knife in 'im."

The other outlaw was already mounting his horse. "To hell with yer shiv. I want the bloody jewels the flash cove prigged from us."

The guard had to be helped inside, where Kathlyn held the man's muffler against his shoulder to stop the bleeding. Mr. Lundquist, having taken on a greenish cast, decided to ride up with the driver, to give her more room. The young couple was no assistance either, Mrs. Tibbett having hysterics and her husband resorting to his flask.

When they reached Lichfield, every one of the inside passengers had to be helped out of the coach. Kathlyn thought her arms would never unbend from holding the guard upright for so long. He'd live, and so would a limp Mrs. Tibbett, taken in hand by the landlady. Mr. Tibbett was another matter, casting up his accounts in the stable yard.

The driver decided to spend the night there. The Mail was supposed to run through the night, with carriage lamps lighting the way. Not without a guard, the driver decided, not with so many miscreants on the road. He did send a messenger on ahead to London, a boy who could ride cross-country, warning the dispatch office of the delay. Kathlyn parted with a handful of coins to see that Lady Rotterdean was also notified.

The next morning they left early with fresh horses, jugs of hot cider, and a substitute guard, who never even drew his pistol at the man standing in the roadway. Mr. Lundquist didn't bother hiding his money this time, and Mrs. Tibbett didn't bother working herself into a tizzy. She just went off in a dead faint across her husband's narrow chest.

Kathlyn was entirely out of patience. "How dare you—" she began when the door opened.

"How do you do, miss. Would you mind if I share the carriage with you good people? My horse seems to have decided that it's not fit weather for man nor beast today, and gone off without me." The stranger drew his heavy frieze coat closer around himself. "I really need to be on my way."

The man looked cold and weary, as if he and his horse had parted company some miles back. Kathlyn edged over on the seat to make room, trying not to crowd Mr. Lundquist overmuch. That gentleman didn't move an inch closer toward the window, muttering about how the driver must have accepted a heavy bribe to put some stray passenger on the waybill. Meanwhile, Mrs. Tibbett was moaning as her husband waved a vinaigrette under her nose. The newcomer looked toward Kathlyn, so she explained about the highwaymen and the posse and the injured guard, remembering to offer the man some of the hot cider. He accepted gratefully, but with shaking hands, from being out in the cold, Kathlyn supposed. He seemed interested in her story, even smiling a bit, but then pulled his hat lower over his eyes and slumped in his corner. He didn't awaken at the next two stops, forcing the others to clamber over his legs.

When they halted for a quick supper, Kathlyn tried to rouse the man. "Mr. Miner, sir? The driver says there won't be another break until morning," she warned, "except to change the horses, of course. You must come into the inn now or you'll go hungry."

When he pushed his hat back, Kathlyn could see that Mr. Miner was not simply weary, but ill. He was ashen in color, with deep lines etched in his face. "I don't wish to intrude, sir, but you must have taken a chill or some hurt from your toss. You should stay here where a physician can be called to attend you."

He tried to smile. "Nothing to worry about, miss. No sawbones." He reached inside his coat with a trembling hand and withdrew a flask and a pound note. "Could you have them fill this?"

Kathlyn did, and bought him a slice of meat pie and a mug of hot coffee with the change. He tried to eat with the same shaking left hand, after Kathlyn unwrapped the pasty for him. She held the mug to his lips while Mrs. Tibbett sniffed her disapproval.

Mr. Miner frowned until the other woman turned away, then told Kathlyn, "You have a good heart, miss. What my mother used to call a shining soul. Thank you." He closed his eyes again.

Kathlyn smiled and set the empty mug on the coach floor. As she reached over, she thought she saw rusty flecks on Mr. Miner's boots and leather breeches. Blood? No, it couldn't be. She was having nightmares from the wounded guard, that was all. Kathlyn quickly picked up her book and tried to read by the last light of day, rather than let her imagination run amok. But Mr. Miner was middle-aged, not young, not old. He was clean-shaven and well spoken. A flash cove? No, only an unfortunate accident victim who refused to see a doctor. She went to sleep, wedged between the wool merchant and the jewel thief.

When she awoke in the morning the carriage was at a standstill and the driver was at the door, shouting, "Gents out."

Mr. Lundquist and Mr. Tibbett stepped down into a snowdrift. Mr. Miner had sweat on his forehead, and seemed surprised to find himself in a coach at all.

"He's too ill to get out," Kathlyn told the driver.

" 'E'll get a lot sicker iffen we stay stuck 'ere like this. We'll all bloody well freeze to death, beg pardon, miss, iffen we don't lighten the load so's the horses can pull us out. Been snowin' all night, 'n' looks to keep on."

"I'll get down," Kathlyn volunteered, putting her hood up.

Mrs. Tibbett wasn't happy. "You can't leave me here alone with him," she whined. "What if he's contagious?"

"Then my staying with you won't help," Kathlyn

25

replied curtly, setting her book and reticule on the empty seat. "We've all been exposed."

A half-smile flickered across Mr. Miner's face. "Not catching."

Mrs. Tibbett got down, too. The baggage was unloaded and the mailbags, the wheels were dug out, and the carriage hauled back to the roadway. By the time the passengers were allowed back inside, they were cold, wet, and weary. Mrs. Tibbett was crying and Mr. Lundquist was consulting his appointments book, trying to figure how much longer the trip would take at the slower speed they were forced to keep.

"Oh dear," Kathlyn fretted, thinking of her new position.

Mr. Miner spoke softly, only to her. "Don't worry. Your goodness will be rewarded."

He must think she was reading the Bible, Kathlyn realized, following his eyes to her book of Shakespeare's sonnets. She shook her head. Surely while she was waiting for her heavenly reward, she would lose her employment here on earth.

They traveled slowly and cautiously, changing horses more frequently as the beasts exhausted themselves pulling the carriage through the snow. Finally, though, they were just one or two stops away from London. Kathlyn urged Mr. Miner to stay behind, to find medical help. He refused again.

"But, sir, I overheard the driver tell the guard that Bow Street would surely have someone waiting for us in London, what with the delays and the holdup we reported."

"Bow Street, eh?" He acknowledged her warning with a chuckle that changed to a choking cough. When he could speak again, he said, "They're naught but a pack of hound pups chasing their tails. The old fox has one more trick up his sleeve."

Playing dead wasn't a very good trick, Kathlyn thought sadly, especially if the fox wasn't pretending. The coach clattered into the inn yard in London, and the door was wrenched open by a spotty-complexioned young man demanding to search the carriage in the name of the law. Not a good trick at all.

Chapter Four

$\mathcal{S}$now covered the inn yard, so Mrs. Tibbett had to be carried across, sobbing on her husband's thin shoulders. Kathlyn thought weeping an excellent idea, if she only had time for such an emotional display. She didn't. She had to get to Lady Rotterdean's in Berkeley Square. The representatives of Bow Street had other plans.

"You wish to do what? I told you I just met the man when he got on the coach. You've turned my reticule inside out, searched my luggage and my cloak pockets. I do not know what you are looking for, but I absolutely refuse to let you—or the landlady, as you so courteously offered—search my person. No, I won't. I've been held up, snowbound, and seated next to a dying man for days. Now you tell me he was a mastermind thief who should have had a fortune in jewels with him, and you won't get paid until you find them. Well, I won't get paid until I find Berkeley Square, so I would appreciate the return of my possessions, on the instant. Please."

Kathlyn was wrong; she did have ample time for hysterics, especially when the younger, spotted Runner threatened to take her off to Bow Street if she did not cooperate with their investigation. The underage, over-zealous jobbernowl was about to get a display of fireworks that would put Vauxhall Gardens to shame. Then the other Runner returned with some hot tea for her. He was older, almost grandfatherly with his silvered hair, spectacles, shuffling gait, and kindly smile. She might even have been happy to see such a solid, reliable figure, if not for his distinctive red waistcoat.

"You've got to forgive Nipperkin, Miss Partland," he was saying, nodding his head in the youth's direction. "That's not his name, neither, which is Ned Ripkin, but I call him Nipperkin on account of him having so much to learn. I'm training him up for the job, just like I would my own boys, see? And my name is Dimm, Jeremiah Dimm. That's my name, not my brain, I always say." He gave a courtly bow, which Kathlyn returned with a nod of her head, sipping the hot tea.

"Now, Nipperkin here, he don't understand women. Me, I spent twenty-odd years with my dear departed Cora, bless her, and some were right odd, I swear. But then I had my daughter with me, and my sister, and her daughters, and *their* daughters, so you see, I understand women, as well as any man can. Reasonable creatures, females. You better write that down, Nipperkin, so you don't forget. Now, I figure that if I explain the situation, a reasonable person such as yourself, miss, being as sensible and law-abiding as my own girls, will help us what has to conduct this investigation."

Kathlyn nodded again and agreed to listen. She had to, lest he think her as addlepated as Mrs. Tibbett, or as guilty as Mr. Miner.

"It's like this," Inspector Dimm began, sitting down to rest his feet while he consulted his Occurrence book. "Bow Street's been after a ring of jewel thieves for years, and finally caught up with your Mr. Miner."

"He's not my anything," Kathlyn insisted.

"He's not Harry Miner neither. Harry Minestere, he was born, but he got dubbed Harry the Diamond Miner from being so successful at his chosen profession. But his luck ran out last month when he was arrested with a pouch full of stolen gems. His gang came and broke him out while they was waiting for the Assizes, though. Harry grabbed up the evidence and took it along. The guards saw it, afore he locked them in their own cell. Downy cove, your friend."

"He's not my friend. He was sick, is all."

"As you say, ma'am, and I'm sure you're right. Anyways, we know he had the jewels. The gang must of had a falling-out over sharing the booty, 'cause the local magistrate reported a dead thug name of Peters, killed by a pistol ball. We know Harry didn't split with his partners, or they wouldn't of held up your coach looking for him, now would they? And the diamonds wasn't in his pockets. So where are the sparklers, I want to know?"

"He hardly left the coach."

" 'Xactly," Inspector Dimm agreed proudly, like her father when one of his students had mastered the fourth declension. "And you were the one he spoke to, what brought him coffee." The Runner held up a weathered hand. "Now, I'm sure you acted out of the goodness of your heart, Miss Partland, a decent, God-fearing lady like yourself, doing as you ought. Why, I'd want my own girls—did I tell you I have two granddaughters? Pretty as pictures, both—to be as kind to strangers in need. And I'm sure you had nothing to do with Harry Miner, but I gots to make sure, you see, or my superior will have my hide. Not very accommodating chap, the governor. This way, I've seen your boney-fides." He pointed to Lady Rotterdean's letter, from Kathlyn's reticule. "So as soon as Mrs. Lambert here has her look-see, we can all go about our business."

"If your business is bothering innocent citizens, you should be ashamed of yourself, Mr. Dimm." Still, she went behind the screens with the landlady and let that woman pat the seams of her clothing. She even took her heavy black braid down, so the woman could see she hadn't any gold candlesticks or such hidden away.

At last she was free to go, with Mr. Dimm's apologies. "It ain't just the jewels we're after, neither, miss. We want to get those partners of his, a pair of cutthroat killers if there ever was. They killed one of the goalers, and now they've held up a Royal Mail coach and shot the guard. The governor wants them found something fierce. If you think of anything useful, you can find me through Bow Street. Oh, and there's a reward for information."

Here was the second man speaking of rewards, when all Kathlyn wanted was to find her warm bed, even if Lady Rotterdean made her sleep in the attic. She wanted dry shoes, her fair wage, and the satisfaction of teaching young minds—that would be enough reward. She didn't want recompense here or in the hereafter for befriending a dying man, and she didn't want to think that she might know anything worth Bow Street's coins. Mostly Kathlyn did not want any more adventures.

But she was still lost in the dark and it was still snowing. Oh dear.

Thank goodness, there was a more brightly lighted road up ahead at last. Kathlyn shifted the grip on her suitcase—now she had blisters on both hands—and headed toward the lamps, her head down to avoid the stinging pellets of wind-driven snow. So she didn't see the two men standing at the entrance to an alley, and walked right into them.

"Well, well, what have we here? Must be a lost little hen, come to roost. Don't worry, chicky, you've found two fine gamecocks to keep you warm." The man thought his wit was hilarious. He slapped his thigh and pounded his friend on the back. The friend fell down in the snow. Kathlyn kept walking toward the lights, faster.

The men came after her. She could hear the crunch of their footsteps, like the sound of a crypt opening. She hurried as fast as she could on the slippery surface.

31

"Naw, Fred, it's a Christmas present from me da, come a bit late. Here I was thinking the old codger'd gone and forgot his favorite son."

"Your dad tossed you out two years ago," Fred gibed, "and he never would have shared a tender morsel like this. I say it's a pretty little fish." He reached an arm out and snagged Kathlyn's cloak. "And she's almost on my hook."

Unable to go farther, Kathlyn turned to face her assailants. "You should be ashamed of yourselves," she blustered so they wouldn't see how frightened she was. "Harassing innocent women. You're inebriated, that's what. And you'll feel great remorse tomorrow, I'm certain."

"That's nothing to what I'm feeling now, sweetings," Fred crowed, his hand grabbing for her breast.

Kathlyn screamed and swung her valise, clipping him on the knees. Fred went down, expanding Kathlyn's vocabulary. She didn't stay to ask for definitions, but dropped her bag and ran. She didn't see that the other man was following her, and she didn't see that she was at a crossing, with a curricle and pair coming straight at her.

Courtney saw it all. He pulled back on his bays, praying they wouldn't slip and break their legs on the icy roadway. If anything happened to his horses, those dirty dishes had even more to answer for than bothering a female who should have known better than to be out alone after dark. The horses stopped, the female ran past, but now both men were loping after her. Courtney cursed at not having his tiger with him, but he never took the groom to Kensington to carry tales. The cattle might stand on their own, but by the time Courtney managed to clamber down from the curricle, those two blackguards would have the woman up some alley or in a recessed doorway.

The viscount backed the curricle and joined the chase.

When he came upon the slower man, he flicked his whip, catching the dastard on the ear.

The other man wasn't so fortunate. The whip coiled right around his neck, dragging him off his feet and almost under the carriage wheels.

Courtney recoiled the whip, snapping it a time or two. The noise made the horses nervous, but not nearly as nervous as it made the two men, now whimpering and scrambling to safety. "Get out of my sight, you muckworms, and don't let me see you again. Next time I'll use my pistol instead." He patted his side pocket, where a pistol would be, if he carried one. When he was sure the men were gone, he turned to the female. He couldn't see her face in the dark, just a pale oval with wide, frightened eyes. "Deuce take it, what were you thinking of, out here by yourself?"

She'd been thinking of a walk through the park, of course. What did this clunch think, that she was enjoying herself? This day, this night—this life—was growing entirely too vexatious to bear a lecture from a stranger. Still, Kathlyn wouldn't forget her manners. "I thank you for coming to my assistance, sir. Good night." She headed back, into the dark, to fetch her suitcase.

Courtney frowned. The female's voice sounded educated, with no trace of London's guttersnipe accent. He waited for her return. "Are you all right, miss?"

He was pulled up near the lamppost Kathlyn had been running toward, not that it would have provided a safe haven, she saw now, for no one was in sight but this fancy swell. He was too full of himself to get down from the elegant yellow-wheeled carriage to come to her aid, no, not even to lift the suitcase that must have gathered paving bricks while it waited on the sidewalk. Kathlyn looked up, noting that he was a handsome devil, with high shirt points and such an intricate neckcloth that only a man of leisure could take the time to tie it. His gleaming horses likely had pedigrees longer than hers. Heavens, they likely ate better than she did. What did a toff like him care about a girl like her? "Thank you, my lord. I am quite well." She bobbed a curtsy as best she could with her mantle now sodden around her ankles and the suitcase dragging down her arm. She turned her back to him again.

Devil a bit, Courtney thought, only a conscienceless cad would let a female walk off unprotected into such a night, even a female as prickly as this one. "Miss, are you near your destination?"

Kathlyn paused. "To be quite honest, I am not sure. I thought someone on this street ahead could direct me. Perhaps you could tell me if I am properly headed toward Berkeley Square."

What could such a draggletailed miss have to do with the cream of Mayfair society? They didn't even let their servants wander unaccompanied. "The east side or the west side of the square?" he probed.

Kathlyn bit her lip, but set the valise on the pavement again, thankfully. "I cannot say. I am looking for Lady Rotterdean's house." When he didn't respond with more than a raised eyebrow, she added, "I'm to be governess to her daughters, but there was a mix-up in the coach schedule."

"Ah." Now Courtney understood. In fact, now he could almost write the unfortunate female's biography, he thought. She was someone's poor but proper relation, fresh from the country. There was no dowry, of course, or she'd be sent to the local assemblies to snabble a husband, instead of being sent to London to work. Oh, and she must be a plain female, for Lady Rotterdean wouldn't have hired a dasher, not with Rottenbottom known to have wandering eyes. Courtney pitied the poor girl, he really did, and acknowledged to himself that he was committed to seeing her safely to a barren, bone-wearying existence—that was still better than what could happen to her on the streets. He gestured with his whip. "It's about six blocks in that direction. It's not out of my way. May I offer you a ride?"

Kathlyn had seen his lip curl at her admission that she was in service. Six blocks were nothing. She'd crawl on her hands and knees, pushing her portmanteau with her nose, rather than accept begrudged favors from any aristocratic jackass. She made a deeper curtsy this time, to show what she thought of his condescension. "Thank you, my lord, but I'll just be on my way."

There was her back again, blast! The female wouldn't last long in service, not with the hauteur of a duchess. She wouldn't last long in the dark either, he reluctantly conceded, turning the carriage again to follow her.

Sure enough, at the very next block, the black-cloaked female was wrestling with a street urchin over possession of her valise. The young cutpurse was turning the frigid air blue with his curses, but the governess was hanging on, retorting with some pithy comments from Horace, if Courtney recalled his schoolboy Latin. In two minutes they'd have half the scum of London crawling out from beneath their rocks, so he used his whip again. The young footpad hied off to the shadows after easier prey, and the viscount held his hand out to the female. "Please, miss, this isn't good for my horses."

His horses? This wasn't good for her tenuous hold on her sanity! In two minutes her remaining wits were going to shatter in a million pieces, a million frozen pieces. She handed up her suitcase, then eyed with uncertainty the high wheels, high steps, and high seat of the sporting vehicle.

"Your hand, miss."

So she put her hand in his gloved one, trying not to wince at the pressure on the blister there, then she was flying through the air, damp skirts and fluttering petticoats and all, onto the seat next to her benefactor, who was even more handsome close up. He had blond curls under his beaver hat, and blue eyes, she thought. A scar on his cheek, following the line of his jaw, gave him a raffish air, magnified when his white teeth flashed her a sudden grin. Oh dear.

"We are going to Lady Rotterdean's, aren't we?"

Chapter Five

*H*igh morals might be cold comfort, but this was worse, having an unprepossessing chit shrink from his helping hand. This dratted woman distrusted him for something he hadn't even thought of doing, hadn't done in the past, wouldn't do in the future, and surely not with some frostbitten, frumpish female. What, did she think he was slavering after her red, wind-roughened cheeks and chapped lips, or her shapeless, bundled body that had about as much weight to it as a weed? He couldn't even see what color eyes she had in the shadow of the hood, nor if she had any hair at all. The only recommendation Courtney found, in fact, was that her nose wasn't dripping. "Yes, miss," he said through clenched teeth, "we are going to Rotterdean House. That's it, straight ahead."

The place he indicated was immense. Immense and very, very dark.

"Surely they cannot all be sleeping?" Kathlyn worried out loud.

Courtney worried louder. "Blast, it's worse. The knocker's off the door." He drove around to the service entry, praying that no one could see Courtney Choate, Viscount Chase, delivering a serving girl like a parcel.

The watchman who peered out at the carriage recognized Quality instantly, of course, even if he couldn't make out the crest in the swirling snow. Otherwise he wouldn't have opened the door at all, not for some trollop come knocking on honest folks' doors. "What's that you're wanting then?" he called to the gentleman, but it was Kathlyn who answered, out of breath from trying not to tangle her skirts or bare her stockings as she climbed down from the curricle, without assistance.

"I'm Kathlyn Partland, the new governess. I was delayed."

The watchman spit into the snow, not far from Kathlyn's feet. "I can see you was."

Kathlyn could feel her cheeks growing warm with a blush, amazing actually, since she hadn't been able to feel an inch of skin anywhere in the last hour. "I did send a message to Lady Rotterdean explaining my plight."

"Well, you're too late. The fambly has packed up and gone to the country."

"But . . . but what about my position?"

"Her nibs said if you wasn't responsible enough to get here on time, you wasn't to be trusted with her babies. In a rare snit, she was, having to look after the hell-spawn herself for an hour, till the agency could send someone over."

Kathlyn's knees were turning to macaroni. Overcooked macaroni. "Perhaps if I follow them, she'll reconsider." And perhaps Kathlyn's few coins would see her there. Another coach ride? She couldn't quite decide which circle of purgatory this situation resembled, possibly the one reserved for ax murderers and assassins. "I can see about it in the morning," she added hopefully.

The man spit again. "Can't stay here, I'm sure. 'Twould be my job, giving houseroom to the likes of you." He jerked his head toward the carriage, where Lord Chase was sorely tempted to use the whip yet again.

Courtney pulled the unfortunate female and her baggage up into the curricle once more, feeling dreadful at her obvious exhaustion and her quivering lip. Just to make conversation till he could get her away from the rum go at Lady Rotterdean's, he said, "I'm sorry I cannot be of more assistance." He gestured toward his cane, on the seat between them. "Bum leg, don't you know."

"I'm sorry," she murmured, but whether for his war wound or for thinking him an unmannered oaf for not handing her up and down, he couldn't tell. Her head was bent, covered with that enormous hood, so he couldn't see if she was crying. He prayed not.

"Don't be sorry. It's a good excuse not to dance with the wallflowers."

Kathlyn was so embarrassed, she couldn't look at him, no matter his efforts. "That awful man will tell Lady Rotterdean—"

"You didn't want to work there anyway."

"Of course I did. It was an excellent position."

"No, I hear the children are such monsters, Lady R can't keep a governess for a week."

She sniffed. "I couldn't keep my job for a day."

Lud, he swore, now the drab was going to turn into a watering pot. The sooner he got her out of his vehicle, the better. "Have you relatives in Town? A friend to stay with while you look for another post?"

"I . . . I have an address that a nice lady at the coaching inn gave me. She said it was a respectable boarding-house, if I ever needed one, with reasonable rates." Kathlyn fumbled with the strings of her reticule, but her fingers were too stiff. They might thaw enough by April to untie the ribbons, she thought. For now she tried to recall the direction. "I believe it was Mrs. McCrory's, on Half Moon Street."

The tired horses still almost managed to rear in their traces, Courtney jerked so hard on the reins.

"You cannot go there."

His authoritarian tone made Kathlyn sit up straighter. "Excuse me?"

"It's out of the question. No place for you at all. I'd sooner take you home with me to—"

Kathlyn gasped. "Stop the carriage this instant. I am getting out."

He looked over to see her starting to descend, with the rig still moving. One hand firmly on the reins, he grabbed the handle of her suitcase with the other so she couldn't leave. "What, are you daft besides?"

"Besides what?" she snapped back.

"Besides as green as a new-hatched tadpole. I am not letting you go to Mother McCrory's."

"*You* are not giving me orders, sir."

Courtney shook his head. "I am sorry, Miss, ah, Partland, I suppose I am too used to doing just that. Let me start over. Mrs. McCrory's is not quite as respectable as you seem to believe."

Yes, but it was the only place Kathlyn knew, and who was he to speak of respectability? "My lord, you have been very kind, and I do appreciate your concern. However, I am one and twenty, and have to make my own way in the world. If you will not take me to Half Moon Street, I can walk, I'm sure."

The viscount took a deep breath, wishing for perhaps the thousandth time that he weren't quite so committed to his own notions of honor. If he weren't a gentleman, by his own definition, he'd dump this plaguish female in the nearest snowbank and get himself and his horses out of the weather. Instead he nodded. "Half Moon Street it is. But don't say I didn't warn you."

Well, there were lights. And carriages, and music, and top-hatted gentlemen conversing on the sidewalk. "Youwarnedme."

"What was that, Miss Partland? You wish to be taken closer to the front door? I didn't quite catch your comment."

"You warned me, you odious man. But you could have mentioned that it was a . . . a . . . ."

He saved her blushes. "Would you have believed me?"

"The woman at the Swan seemed so pleasant, so helpful."

"She was most likely posted there entirely for that purpose, to lure country girls into a life of— But that's irrelevant, miss. It's been a long day."

A long day? If he only knew! Kathlyn's choked-off groan served to confirm his assessment, for her companion continued: "If my mother were in Town, I'd consign you to her care on the instant. Since that is not possible, however, may I offer you temporary lodging at a small place in Kensington with my—"

"No." Kathlyn knew all about gentlemen of the first stare and their small houses on London's outskirts. She might be born yesterday, but it wasn't under a cabbage leaf. The vicar's wife had given her plenty of warnings. And she read books. "That is, no, thank you. But if your mother were in London, where would she stay?"

"Why, at Choate House, naturally."

"No, I mean a hotel. A proper hotel." Kathlyn thought her finances could withstand one night at a tonnish establishment. She didn't think her nerves could withstand another setback.

His mother would stay with any of a hundred relations and friends, never in a rented room. "If Mother did find herself at point non plus, I suppose she'd select the Clarendon. But really, miss, you'll do better in Kensington with Mrs. Dawson."

Share a house with him and his mistress? This was worse than anything the vicar's wife had mentioned. "The Clarendon, please."

He sighed. "I don't suppose it would help if I said I was one of the most trustworthy gentlemen in Town? That I have no designs on your virtue? You can ask practically anyone, blast it—begging your pardon. And Mrs. Dawson will certainly vouch for me."

Her narrowed eyes and stiffened chin told him she was recalling tales about the spider and the fly, the fox and

41

the hen, the big, bad wolf. Him? He sighed again. "The Clarendon."

He pulled up at the canopied walkway. A footman in scarlet livery and wig came to assist Miss Partland down, while the majordomo held the carved front door. A groom ran up to lead the horses away. "No, only the lady will be staying."

Not at the Clarendon, she wouldn't. A single female, one bag, no maid, with a regular Goer for escort, could take her business elsewhere.

"I know, you warned me." Kathlyn held her hand out for a lift up, not feeling the blister anymore, not feeling her hand anymore. The footman had disappeared; Kathlyn didn't know what she would have done if her handsome gentleman had disappeared, too. He was a rake, but he was the only solid ground in this sea of catastrophes. Of course, she didn't know what she was to do now anyway. "Perhaps another hotel? If you were to leave me at the corner where no one could think I was with you?"

"No, no more. I am tired and cold and hungry. You look done in, too, and my horses should be stabled."

Kathlyn did note, through her frantic mental search for a solution, that he'd put her welfare ahead of his horses' this time. At this point she was regretting not letting Mr. Dimm and Ripken cart her off to Bow Street. Could she ask his lordship to take her back to the Swan Inn?

"No. It's Kensington or nothing, and no, I shan't stop for you to get down. I refuse to have your death on my hands. Or worse."

It was the worse that worried Kathlyn. She contemplated jumping out of the curricle, but a manaclelike grasp on her wrist convinced her otherwise.

"No, by Zeus, you'll stay put, you troublesome wench. I've never seen such a one for stubborn, irrational behavior. If you've naught but feathers in your cockloft, it's no wonder you couldn't do better than a position at Rottenbottom's."

That didn't sound like the seduction scene from any novel she'd ever read, so Kathlyn relaxed.

Courtney didn't notice. He was aggravated beyond belief, having been reminded of his own dilemma. "Dash it, miss, I am trying to help you. Why can't you trust me?"

Kathlyn mustered what energy she could to answer such a nonsensical query. "Perhaps because I trusted Lady Rotterdean and that friendly woman at the inn. Perhaps because I trusted my father not to die and leave me, my aunt to save me, or the Royal Mail to get to London on time. I even trusted Mr. Miner not to be a jewel thief, so you can see where my judgment is at best somewhat lacking."

Courtney chose to ignore the bit about a jewel thief. The female was disaster enough without more complications. "Surely you cannot blame your father for dying?"

"He could have made some provision for me first. He could have reconciled with his in-laws. But he didn't. His pride wouldn't let him, so here I am, stranded in London at the mercy of strangers. Everyone I know, yes, everyone, has deceived or disappointed me, and now you are asking me to trust a London beau."

"I'm no Bond Street strutter."

"Excuse me, a fine gentleman, with his pampered horses and his elegant carriage. Why, for my entire life I've been taught that a girl cannot trust your kind!"

His kind? That was almost amusing. Courtney could have been Diogenes's last honest man, but Diogenes—Miss Partland this evening—was wearing blinkers. And his cattle were not pampered. Sympathy for the calamity-prone Miss Partland evaporated. She was still a millstone around his neck, however, so he stiffly replied, "I do see your point, but I can only assure you once more that I mean you no harm. My word as a gentleman."

What else but harm could a handsome young man mean for a defenseless female? Then again, what choice did she have? "You have been very kind," she conceded.

"And Nanny will be kinder yet. That's Mrs. Dawson, my old nursemaid."

"Your nursemaid?" Kathlyn could feel tears welling in her eyes, she was so relieved. She sniffled a few times.

Courtney handed over his handkerchief. Deuce take it, the plaguey chit wasn't going to start bawling now, when they were almost to Nanny's place, was she? "Yes, my retired nurse. She wanted to be near her married daughter and grandchildren, so I purchased a house in Kensington. I visit her frequently, but I rarely spend the night."

"You don't?" The heavenly host might have been singing the Hallelujah Chorus, his words were that sweet to Kathlyn's ears. "And you really have no evil intentions?"

Hell and damnation, what would it take to convince this female that he didn't prey on innocents? Deuce take it, he didn't prey on anyone! And her tears were falling in earnest now, blast it. He patted her back awkwardly. "One leer and Nanny'd comb my hair with a footstool."

She gave him a tremulous smile that made her almost pretty, from what he could see in the shadows of her hood. "Then I'll go to Kensington."

Go? They were almost there, the peagoose. Still, she wasn't crying anymore, so Courtney decided to let her believe the decision was hers. "Better the devil you know, eh?"

"But I don't know you, sir. You've never given me your name."

He bowed slightly over the reins. "Courtney Choate, Viscount Chase, at your service, ma'am."

Kathlyn thought he might have muttered "Damn it all" at the end.

Chapter Six

"It's snowing, you great looby. What do you mean leaving a girl out in the street with your horses? Bring her in, m'lord. Bring her in." Nanny Dawson hustled the viscount back out the door, clucking her tongue. "Since when did I ever turn away a friend of yours? As if I would now, in your very own house. Yes, yes, I know it's my home, and you wouldn't bring a guest in without asking, but the poor child must be half frozen to death."

"She's not a child, and she's not a friend. She's simply someone who needs help."

Nanny stood in the doorway, her woolen shawl protecting her head from the weather, while the viscount limped over to the curricle. "And weren't you always bringing me those injured creatures to mend?" she asked.

Kathlyn felt just like a battered, broken-winged sparrow, one the cat wouldn't drag home, much less a titled gentleman. Still, the cozy figure in the lighted doorway was like a welcoming beacon to warmth, sustenance, safety.

Nanny was a whirlwind in the little parlor, taking off Kathlyn's cloak, adding more coal to the fire, pushing an old dog off the chintz-covered sofa so Kathlyn could

45

sit closest to the hearth. While Courtney was seeing to his horses, Mrs. Dawson bustled back and forth to the kitchen, the closet, the bedrooms, chattering on nineteen to the dozen.

"What is this world coming to when no one watches over innocent young lambs?" She added another dash of rum to the china teapot. "To ward off the chill. Or would you rather have sherry? I'll just set out some of both for you, dearie. And there's my good lamb stew heating up. They never do feed a body right at those posting houses, do they? Five days on the road, you poor poppet? It's no wonder you're all afrazzle." She fetched another quilt to put over Kathlyn's feet, and refilled the glass of sherry.

"I'll get Little George to make up a fire in the master bedroom as soon as he's done helping his lordship with the horses. George is my man-of-all-work that Master Courtney thought I needed. Protection, he calls it, but seeing how George is deaf and dumb, I don't know how much help he'd be. Still, no one else would hire him, and he does carry the coal upstairs for me."

Nanny brought in the stew and a bottle of brandy, then started to unbraid Kathlyn's wet hair while she ate. "I call it the master bedroom," she went on as if there were no interruption, "because I keep it nice in case Master Courtney wants to stay over, but he seldom does, and he won't tonight, so you needn't worry about your reputation, dearie."

Kathlyn wasn't worried about anything, her reputation or her tomorrow or where she was going to sleep. One more sip of the hot tea laced with rum—more like rum laced with tea, by now—and she'd sleep right there, on the spaniel-smelling sofa. Nanny put another blanket over her.

"You did as you ought," the older woman told the viscount when he came in from the carriage mews behind the small row house, stamping snow off his boots. "But then, you always do." She took away an empty dish whose remains looked suspiciously like his favorite lamb stew, nodding toward the mound on the couch. "Poor dear looks worn to a shade."

She looked like a ragamuffin to him, with a comforter pulled up to her reddened nose, black hair every which way on a towel, and skin the color of the snow he was still brushing off his pant legs. "You don't think she's ailing, do you?"

"No, a few days in bed will see roses back in her cheeks, I'm sure."

Mrs. Dawson's words roused Kathlyn from her stupor, not enough to sit up, but enough to mumble through the blankets over her face, "No, I have to go to the agencies tomorrow, to find a position and a place to stay."

"You'll do no such thing, miss. You have years ahead of you to be a governess. I won't hear of you starting until you've had a good long rest. Why, you might have taken a chill, isn't that right, my lord?"

Courtney was sipping his brandy, standing on his bad leg, still in his damp clothes. No one was going to invite him to sit by the fire, he was beginning to realize, or offer him stew or sympathy. "You'll find that you cannot tell Miss Partland anything, Nanny. She has to do things her own pigheaded way."

Kathlyn couldn't let such an insult pass over her, lest Mrs. Dawson think she was an obstinate, ungrateful chit. She sat up, pulled the quilt down, and opened her eyes. "I'm sure Mrs. Dawson's advice is sensible and well founded, not simply an ultimatum issued out of a misguided feeling of superiority."

"Ah, coming the soldier with you, was he? That's what comes of sending boys off to war, I always say. You spend a lifetime smoothing the rough edges off the little hellions, and the army puts them back. Give his lordship time with gentler folks, he'll come around."

Courtney didn't even bother defending himself or the

army. Nanny was still riled that he'd gone off to war, he knew, outraged that he'd come home injured. She blamed Lord Wellington personally for not looking after her nursling better.

"I thought that kind of arrogance was bred in the blood," Kathlyn noted, still smarting from the viscount's ill opinion of her. Pigheaded indeed. She glared at him.

"I—" Courtney got no further. The chit had the most glorious black-rimmed, blue eyes he'd ever seen. They were shadowed with weariness, but still flashing with spirit and little dancing flecks. And all that black hair must come to past her waist, at least. The girl was too thin, of course, with a pinched look about her, but, by George, Lady Rotterdean must never have seen Miss Partland in person!

Nanny hadn't even noticed his lapse, refilling Kathlyn's cup and retucking the blankets around her. "You want some pride in a lad, dearie, else you've got a man with no strength of his convictions."

Lord Chase's convictions were undergoing a severe trial. At least his blood was warm again.

"And if it's governessing you want to do"—Nanny talked while she toweled those long, silky, black locks— "why, I have just the thing. My daughter Meg is close to being confined with her third child and feeling poorly. I've been watching over the other two, but I'd like to sit more with my girl. Her husband's a law clerk and can't stay home with her or the youngsters. The boy is a bright one who should be off to school, but his mam can't part with him. And my little Angela is ready to learn her letters, I'd guess. So you can look after them a bit in a day or two, while you catch your breath, so to speak."

The good Lord *did* answer prayers. In His own good time, but at least Kathlyn could rest easy for now.

Not so his lordship. Nanny was shoving him into his

greatcoat. "Get on home with you now, our Miss Kathlyn needs her sleep."

The chit hadn't been here an hour, and she was "our" Miss Kathlyn, Courtney thought with a degree of resentment commensurate with the discomfort of a cold, hungry drive back to Choate House.

"I've packed up some of my liniment in a jar," Nanny told him on the way to the door. "You can heat it when you get home. Your stableman will know how, if you can't do it."

The stableman? No one was going to massage Courtney's leg or listen to his troubles? No one was going to make sure he was warm and dry and well fed? Bloody hell, even old Wolfie was curled at Miss Partland's feet while Nanny was tossing out the owner of the house. Courtney fumed, pulling his collar up and his hat down; he'd pulled some rubbishing waif out of a blizzard and now he was yesterday's kippers? And it was still snowing, Courtney observed in silent outrage as he rehitched his horses to the curricle without Little George's assistance. Little George, who had to stoop to pass under the doorframe, was carrying water for "our" Miss Kathlyn's bath. Blast!

Kathlyn slept the night through. She awoke to find herself in a damask-draped bedchamber, in her own cotton nightgown. A weak winter sun was beginning to peek through the pulled curtains, so the storm must be over. A fire was burning brightly in the hearth, and a cup of chocolate rested on the bedside table along with a buttered roll. Kathlyn ate, drank, smiled, and went back to sleep.

Not so his lordship. Viscount Chase ate—cold chicken—and he drank—more brandy than was good for him—but he didn't sleep. Since he hadn't bothered with the liniment, his leg was aching too badly for him to get comfortable. Besides, Courtney had an idea. It was an idea so grand, so marvelously comprehensive, that he couldn't wait to share it. In one fell swoop, one night and an outlay of blunt, he could resolve all of his problems.

Miss Partland needed a position. Courtney needed a mistress. How simple! She was too honorable, or too unyielding, he thought, to go back on her word of confidentiality once given. Furthermore, she didn't know anyone, anyway, so she couldn't gossip. His secrets would be safe.

And she wouldn't need a mask at the Cyprians' Ball, not to hide those magnificent eyes. Instead, Lord Chase decided, there in his study a long way from Kensington, he'd costume Miss Partland like a houri, with her inky hair flowing down her back and a diamond hanging from a chain at the center of her forehead. He'd have her bare governess bones covered in filmy, flowing drapery so no one could think he was too miserly to keep her well fed. Sheherazade, he saw in his mind's eye, with bells on her fingers and her ankles bare. Oh yes, and she'd have a gauze veil over her nose (in case it was still red) and the lower part of her face, adding mystery, allure, and hopefully silence. Perhaps the shrew would even keep her mouth shut, with that caustic tongue in it.

He'd parade her around for everyone to see. No, that didn't match the air castle he was building, not with his limp. He'd arrive late, that was it, and make a grand entrance. The sultan and his odalisque? Too obvious. He'd wear his own dress clothes instead, with a sapphire in his neckcloth, perhaps, if he could find one to match her eyes. No mask, for that would defeat the whole purpose.

A brief appearance would be enough to establish his reputation as a connoisseur of women. Then he could go courting. The viscount was determined to wed this very Season, to be done with clacking tongues and cold baths. He'd find himself an innocent young bride, and he'd make dashed certain of it this time, sweeping some rosy, rounded, sweet little miss off her feet the same night she made her first curtsy at Almack's.

By then he'd be long rid of the maggoty female installed in Kensington. He'd pay Miss Partland off and get her out of London, out of his life, out of Nanny's parlor. He didn't like going home as if he were a tot leaving the candy shop empty-handed. Duty to the downtrodden was well and good, but did it require such instant devotion? Courtney didn't like feeling childishly jealous of his nursemaid's attachment to a foundling either! He only hoped he could act the smitten swain for the occasion of the Cyprians' Ball. Of course he could. Miss Partland wasn't an antidote, and her ill fortune was not entirely her fault. Besides, she could make up for his miserable evening and miserable temper in one night at the Argyle Rooms.

Feeling more charitable, the viscount thought that perhaps he'd send Miss Partland to his mother in Trowbridge when their performance was done. It was respectable and it was far away. Yes, that would serve.

So enamored of his idea was Lord Chase that he didn't think of the impropriety of sending his paramour to act as companion to his mother. Nanny did, along with the evil of ruining a good girl's reputation. She wasn't having any of it.

"But it won't be for real, Nan. Your lamb's virtue is safe as houses, I assure you. And we'll change her name, so no one has to know it was Kathlyn Partland at the ball. One night, and she'll earn a year's worth of governess wages."

" 'Tain't right, and that's all I'm going to say until Miss Kathlyn wakes up. She won't do it, so I can save my breath. She's a good girl, our Miss Kathlyn."

"Well, I aim to try, and I'll wager she accepts the offer. She must feel some gratitude to me for bringing her here, and she needs the blunt. Besides, her life must have been so dull, she'll jump at the chance for an adventure! It's not as though anything interesting ever happens to impoverished tutors' dowerless daughters."

Chapter Seven

$\mathcal{I}$t wasn't snowing, but it was so cold, the Thames was freezing over. And hell would freeze over, too, before Kathlyn Partland accepted such an outrageous offer.

Courtney had had to wait until late afternoon to see Miss Partland alone. Clucking her tongue and muttering about men having muscles where their brains should be, Nanny went off to visit her daughter. Kathlyn was on the sofa again, a blanket over her knees. Her hair was braided and coiled at the back of her neck, and she wore a high-necked, low-fashioned gown whose shapelessness was as unattractive as its muddy color. Very governessy indeed, except for the spots of high color on her ivory cheeks.

The viscount was being polite, inquiring for her health and fetching the tea things. He thought he was being subtle, too.

Kathlyn thought he was being a clunch. "You wish to hire me to be an actress? My father would have a stroke. Of course, my father did have a stroke or I wouldn't be in this position. But no, of course not. Performing in public is not a respectable occupation, you must know."

"Yes, but this is only for one night, Miss Partland." He

was seated next to her on the sofa so they could share the plate of scones. He tried to look sincere. 'Struth, he was sincere. "One night, that's all I ask of you."

Kathlyn stirred her tea, pretending to deliberate for courtesy's sake. "I did take part in amateur theatricals once at the vicarage. Precisely what character is it that you wish me to portray?"

"My mistress."

The dog had sense enough to run away.

"I have never seen such a female for flying into the boughs," Courtney said, rubbing his cheek. "I said you'd be performing a role for one night, not performing naked dances on top of a table. I did *not* proposition you actually to *be* my mistress. By Jupiter, nothing was further from my thoughts."

"Of course, I'm sorry. You did say an assumed role." Kathlyn was aghast at her actions. She'd never struck a gentleman before in her life. Now the impression of her hand was vivid on his cheek, right above the scar. "Oh dear, did I hurt you badly?"

"Nothing I didn't deserve, Miss Partland, for putting my proposal to you so baldly. Truly, don't give it another thought." He took a bite of his scone to show he wasn't permanently damaged, even though his jaw ached like the very devil. How could such a wispy wench pack such a wallop? "More tea?"

"Thank you." Kathlyn managed to hide her mortification behind the teacup, where she didn't have to say anything more. He really had been kind. Why could she not be civil in return? Perhaps because she sensed his disapproval of her. Lord Chase treated her like a misdelivered package, so of course he didn't want her for his mistress. He didn't even want her in his house. Furthermore, no man as handsome and well set up as the viscount would ever have to hire a mistress, pretend or otherwise. Women must be falling all over themselves to volunteer for the position.

"Why?"

"Why what?"

"Why do you need to hire someone to pretend to be your mistress? It makes no sense."

"Life makes no sense." He crumbled half a scone, to tempt the dog back to his side and to avoid meeting her curious blue gaze. "I do not have a mistress. I do not want a mistress. Yet for reasons of my own, I need to present one at an upcoming social event."

"Can you not ask one of your friends' sisters? A society miss?"

"No, the situation does not require a young lady, just a ladybird. An alluring, attractive female who would make every man in the room pant with desire and drool with jealousy."

Kathlyn almost dropped her teacup. "Me?" He didn't even like her!

"With a cloth over your face, naturally." Courtney wasn't about to tell the poker-backed governess that he found her exquisite. She was too skinny for his taste anyway. "And lots of gauzy stuff to hide your, ah, figure."

Kathlyn scowled. So much for a crumb of approval. "So why won't you find your *belle de nuit* among the demimonde? Surely one of those women would know how to—"

"That needn't concern you. My reasons are none of your business."

Kathlyn swirled the leaves in the bottom of her cup. "My business isn't treading the boards either, in case you have forgotten. It's teaching little children."

"With my blunt you can start a school somewhere. You can't want to be a servant in some rich man's house."

"I don't have a choice."

"You don't have a job either, do you? Nanny says you went out to an agency today, despite her advice, despite her generosity in offering you a home here for as long as you wish."

55

"Mrs. Dawson has been everything kind, but I cannot accept her charity."

"Charity? You'd be doing her a favor by staying while her daughter is confined." He brushed that aside, with the crumbs from his fingers. "What luck did you have?"

"None, you must know." She studied those tea leaves for inspiration. "I have no references."

Now he studied his fingernails. "My mother might be able to write you a good character. She lives in Trowbridge but has a wide circle of friends and correspondents here in town and across the country. Surely one of them knows someone in need of an excellent governess."

"But I do not know your mother. Why would she do that for me?"

"Actually she'd be doing it for me, if I asked her."

"And you would ask her in exchange for . . . ?"

"One night."

"That's blackmail!"

"Not at all, I'm merely sweetening the pot." She looked at him without comprehension. "Upping the ante, don't you know, making my offer more attractive."

Well, it was getting more attractive by the moment. A year's worth of wages and a recommendation . . . "Nanny would never approve."

Nanny *didn't* approve, but Miss Partland didn't have to know that. "Nanny would gladly pardon our little deception if she thought it would help me win the affections of a blushing debutante. She'd do anything to see me married so she'll have more babies to coddle."

Kathlyn smiled at last. "Oh, I see. You're trying to make some respectable female jealous! And of course you do not want to arouse expectations in some other girl."

"Well, you might say so." Miss Partland might say the moon was made of green cheese, if she agreed to his plan. If it made her happy to think this was some romantic subterfuge, fine. Then maybe she'd stop being so analytical, so inquisitive, so schoolmarmish.

But Kathlyn was a schoolmarm, or would like to be. "But why a mistress?" she asked to Courtney's aggravation. This was already a devilish conversation to be having with a straitlaced spinster.

"Why not?"

"Because no girl is going to be impressed by a womanizer."

Maybe she actually did think the moon was made of green cheese. "You are incredibly naive if you believe that, Miss Partland. Don't you know that rakes are supposed to make the best husbands? Some young miss is dreaming this very moment of her evening at Almack's and the libertine who will reform for love of her."

"The poor girl."

Kathlyn took another scone, but she did agree to think about the viscount's proposal overnight. She owed him that much.

"Mrs. Dawson, do you think it is terrible to do something wrong if you do it for good reasons?"

Nanny didn't stop chopping the vegetables for dinner. "I suppose it depends on how right and how wrong." Chop, chop. "Like if a man steals a loaf of bread to feed his starving children. The law says it's a crime, but I say there's nothing more sinful than children going hungry." Chop, chop. "There, you can roll that dough a tad thinner, dearie. A' course, if every hungry soul stole a loaf, then the baker's children would have none." Chop. "But if you're thinking about his lordship's mad notion of making you his convenient for one night, well, I can't begin to comprehend his reasons, good or bad." Whack. Whack. "It's a male thing, and we females will never understand." From the violence of Nanny's chopping, it was a good thing Lord Chase and his male thing were not present. She slammed the oven door, rapped Little George's knuckles for tasting the soup stock, and nudged the old dog out of her way with her foot. "Then again, if

Master Courtney says no harm'll come, I suppose he's in the right of it."

Then again, Kathlyn thought, Nanny Dawson believed his lordship could walk on water. He couldn't, no more than he could make his reasons for this odd start seem logical. But he hadn't given any reasons, Kathlyn recalled, he just hadn't disagreed with her conclusions.

Making another woman jealous made no sense, no matter what Lord Chase said about reformed rakes. No woman could be foolish enough to think a gold band changed a tiger's stripes. No, he had to have another reason for this proposed farce of dull Miss Partland playing the dasher, and Kathlyn was desperate to know it. If his lordship had the remotest semblance of an honorable motive, Kathlyn could accept his offer. She could accept his money, enough to start a school of her own somewhere, and she could accept his mother's reference to attract students. In good conscience she could have a short respite here at Mrs. Dawson's, helping around the house and entertaining the grandchildren. She wiped flour off her hands, thinking she'd never been so comfortable, so cozy, since her mother's passing six years ago.

She wanted to stay, if only for the few weeks. And she was sorely tempted to get dressed up and attend her first fancy ball. It wouldn't be quite the thing, of course, but the closest Kathlyn Partland was liable to get to high society in her lifetime. She wasn't even worried about the viscount's going beyond the line. If he didn't hold her in aversion, he certainly didn't give the appearance of a gentleman wanting to hold her, period.

Kathlyn was beginning to recognize that look. She'd seen it again this very morning, at her second foray to the employment agencies. A prospective footman in one of the waiting rooms gave her such a particular stare that the agency's proprietress cancelled both of them from her appointments book.

The second agency had one position available, at a "difficult" household. Desperate, Kathlyn had gone on to be interviewed by the master of the house, to find the only difficulty was getting out of there with her clothing intact. Viscount Chase's disreputable offer was better than that, or would be if she could only understand it.

The whole thing came down to his motives. If his lordship had been aboveboard and said, for instance, that he had a wager with some chums about bringing an Incognita to the ball, she might have understood. London gentlemen were known to bet on how many birds landed on a fence rail, or who could walk backwards faster. But he hadn't been aboveboard, he hadn't trusted her with his objectives, so she couldn't trust him. If she couldn't trust him, she couldn't believe his promises about safeguarding her identity or providing for her future. But why? Always, why?

Why would an honorable gentleman—and Nanny Dawson swore the viscount was a decent man, a hero even—resort to such subterfuge? If there was a wager, a dare, or even a foolish young lady of his own circles, why didn't Lord Chase simply hire himself a courtesan? With his money and address, he could have his pick of the muslin company. Kathlyn had heard about the ranks of the Fashionable Impure, the elegant, sophisticated women of the world who knew how to bat their eyelashes, wave their fans, and please a man. In Lord Chase's wildest imagination, he could not think Kathlyn was one of them, in her brown bombazine and tight braids and one journey away from home. He didn't think she had the sense God gave a duck, so why would he think she could flirt with his friends?

Why, with his good looks, didn't he have a willing *chérie amour* of his own? All he needed to do was flash his dimples and bright smile to have hearts flutter. The hearts of foolish women with romantical notions, Kathlyn amended, taking off her apron. Of which she was not one, of course. She shook her head. It must be, as Nanny said, one of those incomprehensible male things, like wearing shirt points so high, they could put one's

59

eyes out, or carrying canes for no reason. But Viscount Chase had a reason. It must be . . . his war wound!

Oh, the poor man!

It was a male thing, Courtney acknowledged, like having the fastest Thoroughbred, the sleekest rig, the best aim at Manton's shooting gallery. It was competitiveness, making the other chaps jealous. It was sheer masculine pride. He had to have that woman on his arm at the Cyprians' Ball. He'd never felt this way, this burning need of possession, not even squiring Adelina Marlowe about before they were engaged. Hell, he hadn't felt so possessive of Adelina even *while* they were engaged. He had to have Miss Partland—for that one night, he told himself. The female threatened his equilibrium, but not his self-imposed vows, of course.

So he had to raise the stakes even higher. Money did not seem to be the sticking point with the prickly female.

"Miss Partland, I have been rethinking my offer." He was staring at the fire, carefully framing his terms.

"Yes."

"That if you do accept, you'd find yourself at loose ends here in London for the time until the ball. And an intelligent female like yourself, hoping to educate other young minds, would like to visit some of the historic sights, the cathedrals and such, before you go. I would undertake to guide you to all the notable places recommended in the guide books, as part of our bargain, you must know, not that I would impose my company on you."

"I understand. Yes, thank you."

"And, ah, since it could only redound to my credit to have a beautiful woman in my escort well before our appearance at the ball, I would undertake the responsibility and expense of providing a suitable wardrobe."

Kathlyn fingered the worn skirts of her shapeless gown. She shouldn't let a gentleman pay for her clothing, but she couldn't embarrass the poor viscount by looking like a washerwoman. Her funds wouldn't extend so far as a new bonnet, so there was no choice, really. She nodded. "Of course. Thank you. Yes."

"And you'll need a maid, naturally, to help care for your belongings."

A maid? Kathlyn had never had a servant to wait on her in her life. Her brow creased.

The viscount rushed on, "That way you'll have more time to devote to Nanny's grandchildren, when we're not out sightseeing, rather than having to be ironing and mending. And the woman could be a help to Nanny betimes."

"Why, how very thoughtful, my lord. Yes."

"Yes? Then you accept? You'll do it?"

"Yes, my lord, I said so."

He wiped his brow. "You drive a hard bargain, Miss Partland, but I don't regret it. And you won't either. Don't forget, it will be Kitty Parke the rumormongers gossip about."

Kathlyn was distressed. "What, are you ruining another girl's reputation?"

"No, silly, just changing your name so no one outside this house can identify you. Nanny would never tell and George cannot, so Miss Kathlyn Partland's good name is preserved, and no one in all of London will recognize that she and Kitty Parke are one and the same."

No one except Bow Street's finest investigator.

Chapter Eight

$\mathcal{M}$ore snow, gorblimey. Inspector Dimm's eyebrows had icicles hanging from them, and his nose nigh broke right off when he went to blow it. B'gad, wasn't this winter ever going to end? He was too old for this tomfoolery, the Runner told himself, too old to trek his bunions across town looking for some woman as was no better'n she ought to be. Mostly, he thought, he was too old for the job if he let a prime suspect slip through his fingers just because she was a prime article. Taken in by a pretty face, b'gosh. At his age.

He should have known better than to boast to Ripken about understanding women. No man understood women. Illogical, emotional, tricky beings, females were, not straightforward like men. Even Inspector Dimm's own dear Cora, God rest her soul, could be purring one minute and hissing the next. Of course, she'd never change her manners and her morals overnight, the way the Partland female seemed to have done. How could a man have figured that? Now Dimm was going to look no-account in the young trainee's eyes. And the governor's, if he didn't solve this case.

Dimm had trusted his own intuition and come acropper. Intuition was what a good investigator could rely on when he had no solid facts, but intuition was like a woman, all moods and megrims. Dimm was thinking that mayhaps he should have stayed retired in the country if he was going to make micefeet of his first case back. But life in the shires was too peaceful, too quiet. The only excitement was a bull getting out of its pen, and the only noise was birdsong. How did they expect a fellow to sleep without carts and street-sellers and all-night travelers outside his window? Besides, a parcel of his kin were out in the country now, right on his doorstep with all of their in-laws and all of their infants. Having them all together at Christmas had him hieing back to the city for some solitude. Now he was in the middle of Harry Miner's murder case, a major jewel heist, and a holdup of the Royal Mail.

And he'd made a royal blunder.

Mr. Dimm lit his pipe, wishing he had his aching feet soaking in a tub of hot water instead of sloshing through the foot of slush at the sides of the road. The governor believed his men didn't need to be taking hackneys. The governor also believed every crime had a simple and easy solution, bless his clutch-fisted heart.

The pipe went out in the wind of the street, but Mr. Dimm chewed on its stem anyway. It helped him think. By Harry, he repeated to himself, he'd thought the chit was a lady to her toes. It wasn't like him to be so far afield. Jeremiah Dimm was losing his touch, slipping— no, that was the ice underfoot.

He hadn't been entirely negligent, he reminded himself, at least sending Nipperkin back along the coach route to check out the coaching crew's accounts of when and where Harry Miner left the carriage, if anyone'd seen him leave the inn yards or bespeak a room—anywhere he could have stashed the gems. Nipperkin was also supposed to corroborate the passengers' stories, the girl's in particular.

Ripken got back this afternoon. He hadn't found the jewels, of course, nor any hint of where they might be.

Dimm wasn't surprised that Harry Miner hadn't made it easy for them; he'd stayed out of Bow Street's nets for years. With so much snow on the ground up north, Ripken couldn't search around all the privies, but he did make sure the innkeeps and ostlers along the route knew about the reward for a cache of stolen booty.

Ripken's report on the female was more disturbing. She was Hannibal Partland's daughter, all right, and left on her own when the tutor died recently, as she had said. According to Nipperkin, the local vicar and his wife said that she was also niece to Lady Madorra Bellamy of Manchester. The family had disowned Miss Partland's mother for marrying an impoverished scholar, and Lady Bellamy continued the tradition. Despite having married well, a nabob from the East India Company, Lady Bellamy had made no effort to assist the tutor or his orphaned daughter. Madorra Bellamy, coincidentally or not, was also the lady most recently relieved of her jewels by Harry Miner and his gang.

"And she never onct said she was related." Ripken strode by Dimm's side, not even noticing the slippery patches or puddles, he was so excited to be near to solving his first case.

Dimm just grunted. "I don't recall us asking after her relations, nor saying whose baubles had been filched."

"I say she set out to prig her aunt's sparklers out of revenge, and 'cause she thought her ma'd been cheated of her inheritance."

"Harry Miner stole the diamonds, you paperskull. He had them on him, b'gad. And he'd been operating up north for months. It had nothing to do with revenge."

"But Harry Miner had a wife, we know he did."

Dimm paused to flip through the pages of his Occurrence book, where he kept his notes. "Ursula Miner's got bright yellow hair."

"So she dyed it. You would, too, if you was Harry Miner's widow and had the loot his cutthroat partners was after."

Dimm put away his book and his pipe, now that it was cool. He started walking again. "You said yourself Miss Partland was living with her father, some pence-per-hour tutor. 'Sides, she ain't old enough to be Harry Miner's wife." He shook his head, sending a shower of snow-flakes off the brim of his hat, down his neck. "And she didn't have the stolen property, you booberkin."

"So why're we going to Lady Rotterdean's?"

"To ask Miss Partland about her relatives, of course. And to see if she remembered anything Harry might of said during the coach ride. Maybe the reward'll look more inviting after a week of taking care of some blue-blooded brats. Amazing what discontent can do for the memory."

But Miss Kathlyn Partland wasn't taking care of the Rotterdean rug rats. She wasn't there at all. The only one of the household who was there, a footman left behind to guard the place, wouldn't open the door until he saw the shine of gold. The governor didn't approve of buying information either, but Dimm found it the fastest, easiest way of finding what he needed, especially since he wasn't so fast with his fives anymore.

Miss Partland was supposed to be here—she hadn't lied about that—but she got to London too late to join the family before they left for their country property.

"Deuced convenient, if you ask me."

"I didn't, so shut up, Nipperkin." Mr. Dimm turned back to the guard, with another coin. "The fambly left. So what did you do with Miss Partland?"

"Do? Nothing I could do. Couldn't give her fare to join them 'cause I didn't have any. Couldn't call out a carriage for her 'cause there's no one to drive. 'Sides, Lady Rotterdean hired another female to bear-lead those brats. Would of offered her a bed for the night, mine, a'course," he said with a wink and a leer, " ' 'cept she didn't need it, not with that gentry cove waiting in his carriage. Sporting vehicle, it was, right expensive-looking, and horses with style, too. Real Quality, I could tell. Matched bays, they were."

"Like every other Nonpareil's cattle," Dimm muttered in frustration.

"See, the mort pulled the wool over our eyes," Ripken crowed. "It were all a sham, that prunes-and-prisms act. She had her aunt's jewels all the time. Or else," he expounded, warming to his theory, "she passed the sparklers to her partner at some inn outside Town, and was waiting to get here to claim them from him. That governess rigmarole was only to throw us off the scent."

"No, she was a governess, all right and tight. She had Lady Rotterdean's letter. And don't go off half-cocked about forgeries and such. That watchman said they was expecting her, only she got here too late what with the snow and all. Raw deal for a gently bred female."

"Then where is she now?"

"You finally asked a good question, my boy." Dimm took out his pipe and cleaned it, then refilled it. He didn't bother lighting up, not out in the street, but did some thinking while his hands were busy. Ignoring the flash cove for now, Dimm still figured the female for a governess. "Say she found a place to shelter—"

Ripken snickered. "Warm place, by the looks of it."

"She'd still need a job. We'll try the agencies first."

They split the list in half. Dimm found one employment bureau that had sent Kathlyn Partland out on an interview. She never came back, and they were still looking for someone for the post. Ripken located two agencies where she was remembered, but they'd had no jobs to offer.

The Runners went back to the Swan Inn, to see if Miss Partland had returned there, or if she'd left any baggage behind. Sure enough, her trunk had been picked up by a swell in a yellow-wheeled curricle, with matched bays. He didn't give his name.

"You see?" Ripken was gloating over his ale in the Swan's public room. "The mort said she knew no one in London, but she landed on her feet in a hurry. That was too fast for any light-skirt to find a new protector, and it was snowing. She must have arranged with her lover aforehand, even if she had to toss the gems out the carriage window."

"The other passengers would have noticed." Dimm was looking over the waybills. Miss Partland's name wasn't on any of the recent lists, but Dimm decided to send Ripken north again. The bird was flown, and the overeager youngster was getting on his nerves, seeing criminals behind every bush. He'd never wanted a partner in the first place.

"But I just got back from there, and the roads're like washboards this time of year. My arse is still sore from bouncing in that carriage."

Maybe the next bounce would put some sense into the Nipperkin's brain. At least he'd be gone so Dimm could do his own speculating in peace.

"What are you going to be doing while I'm chasing after the jade?" Ripken wanted to know.

"I'm going to read the newspapers and feed the squirrels in the park."

"While I'm off riding the mails on a fool's errand?"

"Who better to send?"

"The governor ain't going to like it, not by half."

Dimm sighed. " 'Is nibs likes his fellows guarding the coaches. You'll get special commendation, I'm sure. 'Sides, I'll be working, too, you looby, reading those gossip columns to see what nob has set up a new mistress, and watching the carriage paths. Our bloke'll be wanting to show off his new ladybird in the park, especially if he's got a handsome curricle. Horses have to be exercised, even in the cold."

"How will you recognize the matched bays?"

"I won't be looking for the horses, you noddy. I'll be looking for Miss Partland."

"What, do you think she's going to be wearing some dingy old hooded cloak? Not while she's in some rich man's keeping, she won't."

"Didn't I teach you to notice things? How could a

body not recognize that female no matter what she's wearing? Her eyes are like bluebells pressed in a frame. Her skin's like white rose petals, and her hair is like a curtain of black satin."

Ripken whistled. "You noticed all that?"

"I'm old, not dead."

"But what if she's wearing a disguise? You know, dark glasses, a wig?"

"What kind of high flyer wears spectacles? 'Sides, no gent who's paying for that kind of merchandise is going to hide a light under a barrel. I wouldn't. Would you?"

Getting up to make his way out to the departing coach, Ripken grinned. "I ain't an old man. I'd keep her too busy to leave the house."

"There's that, I suppose. But the Cyprians' Ball is coming. She'll be there."

So here Dimm was, freezing his tail to the iron bench by the entrance to the park, pretending that he wouldn't rather be back at his warm little house in Kensington soaking his feet with no one to bother him but the cat. Every once in a while he felt prickles at the back of his neck, as if someone were watching him, instead of vicey versey. But no one was there except the squirrels looking for peanuts.

No, his instincts must be wearing out, gorblimey. He'd have to retire again after this case, and this time not come back even if he did get bored. Iffen an officer of the law couldn't trust his instincts, he shouldn't be in that line of work. And he shouldn't wear a scratchy wool muffler if he was going to get rashes on the back of his neck.

Inspector Dimm's instincts were fine; it was his eyesight that was going. He was indeed being watched, having been followed to the park by two churls getting more churlish out in the cold. The Diamond Mine gang, what was left of it, wanted the ice. Not the ice under the Bow Street Runner's rump, but the diamonds Harry

Miner snabbled out of the magistrate's strongbox before his trial.

After a talk with the stableboy, who was left cursing the day that gallows-cheat ever arrived at the Swan, Miner's ex-partners, Quigley and Sean, had as much information as Dimm. Like Ripken, they figured the girl knew something. She'd asked directions to Rotterdean House, so they went there, almost tripping over the inspector and his assistant. Quigley and Sean waited behind some shrubs until the Redbreasts left. Relieving the Rotterdean watchman of his recent windfall and two of his teeth, they found the same news, that Kathlyn Partland had vanished in a toff's rig.

"Damn, our jewels is gone. You never should of let 'Arry get away," Sean, the shorter cracksman, complained.

"Me?" Quigley cuffed his partner on the ear. "Blockhead, I told you 'Arry was too smart to get on where everyone'd be lookin' for 'im. So now we got to find the female 'e was friendly-like with afore 'e died. Must of told 'er where to find the rocks."

" 'Arry always did like the ladies, but how're we goin' to find one dollymop in all of London? I never thought to get a good look at 'er in the coach, just that old 'Arry wasn't there."

"That's why we pay taxes, you dolt, to let Bow Street do our searchin' for us."

"But we don't pay no taxes, Quig."

That got him another smack on the head. "Shut up and follow the Runners. I'll stay with the old windbag, you follow the young'un. Leave a message at Shippy's if you find anything."

Ursula Miner had a problem: Who was going to lead the way to her diamonds? They belonged to her, no mistake, not to those mawworms who tried to take the loot from Harry because they didn't understand about waiting for the hue and cry to die down before cutting up the gems. Sean and Quigley were nothing but fools. And so was Harry, for thinking he could take off without her.

She missed Harry, Ursula did. He was a real gent. She was sorry she'd turned him in. Of course, she was sorrier she hadn't gotten the reward because he broke out of gaol before being convicted. Well, they weren't going to get away with it, any of them, especially not that little maggot Sean who'd gone and killed Harry. For two bits she'd turn him in to the Runners right now, if she didn't need him to help find the jewels.

He went after the young Runner, but Ursula decided to bide here in the park awhile in her wig and powdered face. The old man was more experienced, she figured; his instincts ought to be good by now. Besides, he looked like a sweet old gent a girl could wrap around her fingers, maybe get some information out of, after she got rid of Quigley.

Gorblimey, Dimm's neck was itchy. Must be the snow trickling down his back.

Chapter Nine

The sun was finally poking out of the clouds, bringing the temperatures from numbing to almost bearable. The wind was only blowing gale force, instead of the cyclones of the past week. Miss Partland's new wardrobe was accumulating apace. She would not embarrass his lordship, according to Nanny and the new maid, Lizzie, so Courtney was able at last to make good on another of his promises. The maid was a neighbor's girl who had a fondness for children and was willing to stay with Nanny's grandchildren while her Miss Kitty was out. She also had a fondness for Little George, "a man what won't argufy with everything a lady says."

There was nothing to stop an excursion to the park, except Miss Partland herself.

"Oh no, my lord, I've been poked and prodded, fitted and fashioned, into a woman of style. Now I wish to broaden my mind. There is a world of history and art right at our doorstep. Surely the park can wait."

So they set out for Westminster and the Tower, Lincoln's Fields and the British Museum. Courtney was thinking that it was amazing what a bit of sunshine could do. London sparkled like a grande dame in her jewels, even if the sooted snow gave the appearance of soiled hems. It was also amazing what a few fripperies could do for a woman's temperament. Very well, Lord Chase had paid enough linen-drapers' bills to outfit the army in Spain, but it was worth it. Miss Partland—he must remember to begin calling her Kitty—was exquisite. That went without saying, with her hair in a new upswept style trailing black ringlets along her ivory cheeks, and her bonnet decorated with silk forget-me-nots that matched the color of her incredible eyes. He was also surprised and relieved to find that her figure in the slim, high-waisted gowns wasn't skin and bones as he'd thought; it was elegantly ethereal, curving delightfully just where it ought.

The big surprise, however, was that Kitty herself was everything charming. She was interested, appreciative, and pleased to share her excitement in the day. The viscount could not have asked for better company. That he'd had to buy it was the only disappointment. While Kitty was cooing like a dove, he was missing Kathlyn's sharp talons, for at least they were honest. Still, if his wealth could turn a harpy like Miss Partland up sweet, it ought to purchase him any bride he selected.

Noting Kitty's sudden concern for his leg, her attention to how he took his tea, her apparent respect for the knowledge he had about the London landmarks, Courtney had to wonder if he was waiting his whole life for an ideal that did not exist. Was he going to have to buy his wife's affection, too, or was there a woman in all of London who could love him for himself? And how was he to know the difference?

There were chaps he knew in his position who went incognito into the countryside, to find an unspoiled bride whose eyes would shine with love, not the color of gold. But he didn't have time for that fustian. He had properties to oversee, his seat in Parliament, his work with the War Office. Besides, he didn't want a milkmaid; he wanted a woman who could take her place with him in

London society, where he was known too well to pretend poverty.

That wasn't all, though. He didn't simply want a bride to fill the position of his viscountess. He wanted one to fill his heart. And he didn't want to be some ambitious female's first choice among the eligible bachelors—he wanted to be her only choice. If he couldn't have that, a love for all time, till death do us part, then he'd been wasting his life. Instead of waiting years for his heart's mate, he could have been enjoying his days and nights with females like Kitty Parke, confound it.

How charming his lordship could be when his leg wasn't paining him. Old Mr. Thistlewaite at home used to be the same, growly with the rheumatics in stormy weather, sweet as a lamb when the sun shone. Or, speaking of lambs, perhaps it was all the flibbertigibbet females making sheep eyes at the viscount that had him in good spirits today. He was so handsome, with the sun on his fair hair and his coat stretched over broad, muscular shoulders, that it was all Kathlyn could do not to make sheep eyes herself.

Whatever the cause, Kathlyn couldn't remember a day she enjoyed more. Why, it was as if all of British history, and some Greek, Roman, and Egyptian as well, was laid out for her perusal. The awesome cathedrals, the impressive seats of the government, the collections of masterpieces, had her nearly speechless in wonder. That would have been enough, but on top of the sight-seeing, Miss Kathlyn Partland felt that she was on top of the world.

Here she was, dressed like a lady, being treated like an equal by this proud, elegant gentleman who was turned out to a shade, drove to an inch, and was the envy of everyone they passed. And he was being kind.

This was beyond anything Kathlyn could have imagined in her most vivid daydream. Of course, she wasn't about to let her head get turned by one day's pleasure. Her fine new feathers still had no nest of their own, she still needed a position, and the viscount was still worlds above her touch, no matter how kind he was acting. She wouldn't let herself forget that his courtliness was an act.

Lord Chase needed Kitty Parke to prove his virility to his circle of acquaintances. What woman would enter a marriage knowing that she'd have no children, that her husband's estates would be left elsewhere when no heir was forthcoming, that she would never experience the joys of the marriage bed? Only the most ambitious, who wouldn't mind a lifeless marriage of convenience. Or a female in love, who was going to be monstrously disappointed.

Kathlyn wouldn't think about the morality of duping some innocent miss into throwing her cap over a windmill with missing parts. Then again, perhaps his lordship suffered a temporary handicap and his marriage would be normal. She hoped so, for his sake, for if there was anything she knew about the nobility, it was their fixation on assuring their successions. She couldn't ask Nanny about Lord Chase's problem, nor, heaven forfend, the viscount himself, the poor, brave man.

She smiled at him, and he patted her gloved hand in the crook of his elbow, pointing out his favorite Turner seascape. Once Kathlyn was in his employ, it seemed, he'd become kindness itself, treating her with as much care and respect as he accorded Nanny. Why, he'd even insisted on purchasing for her an entire wardrobe, not just a few ensembles for public notice.

Back home she'd have been thrilled with a new nosegay to refurbish her old bonnet. Now most of her old clothes were being given to charity, for not even Lizzie would wear them, and Kathlyn was to have everything new from the skin out. No one was going to see her bedclothes, yet Lord Chase convinced her that the modistes would gossip inordinately if she didn't have gossamer nightgowns. She might freeze, but she would look the part of mistress even in her sleep. And he was right, fancy underpinnings of silk and lace did make a woman feel prettier, more feminine. Her favorite of the new clothes was the pelisse of celestial blue she wore now, with its bleached rabbit-fur lining. Let those true birds of paradise enjoy their scanties; Kathlyn thought there was nothing more heavenly than being warm.

What the cloak couldn't warm, the viscount's approving regard could. Of course it was all for show, Kathlyn reminded herself again, but she was determined to repay his kindness by being the female he needed. If only she knew what that was.

"Shall we take a turn about the park now, Kitty, before heading back to Nanny's? It's the fashionable hour to see all the nobs on the strut."

"And to be seen, according to Lizzie. But, my lord, before we join the public parade, before you have to introduce me to your friends, perhaps we should go somewhere for a more private conversation. You see, I do not know how a mistress behaves." She was blushing like a schoolgirl. "In public. That is, I don't know how a mistress conducts herself in private either, of course."

And he did? Well, yes, he'd seen enough high flyers on various friends' arms. On the way to Gunther's he considered the matter. Some of the doxies were openly flirtatious, both with their escorts and with every other man in the vicinity. Looking for their future protectors, he assumed. No, he'd not want Kathlyn acting so brass-faced. "No flirting with other men," he iterated.

Kathlyn thought it made sense for a mistress's loyalties to be engaged along with her other attributes. She nodded.

Courtney thought of how many light-skirts he'd heard cajoling their lovers for another expensive bauble. There was no pretending to anything but a sordid business arrangement when the jades withheld their affections until their protectors held out another glittering bribe. He didn't think Miss Partland was grasping, not when he'd had to encourage her to purchase even the minimum amount of gowns, and she insisted on purchasing her gloves and stockings at the Pantheon Bazaar with Lizzie, instead of at the more expensive modistes. Still, most women were inveterate shoppers. Now that Kitty had a taste of lavish spending, she might crave it as a steady diet. "Don't get greedy."

Kathlyn thought she had everything she could need for the next lifetime. How could any man be more generous, and how could any woman ask for more? She nodded again. "What else?"

Why bother mentioning that a mistress should be discreet? Miss Partland had as much to lose in exposure as Courtney did. Instead he told her, "Don't show jealousy. It's unbecoming." He remembered one of Algie's ladybirds who threw a tantrum—and a candelabrum—when Algie was going off with himself and Woody to a mill, instead of dancing attendance on her.

Kathlyn thought he meant she should turn her back when his attentions turned to women of his own class. Of course, she would. That's what this was all in purpose of, wasn't it, finding him a bride? "What else?"

"No scenes, no nagging. If there's anything a man doesn't want in a mistress, it's aggravation. He can get that from his wife."

Public spectacles were the mark of vulgarity; carping, the trait of a shrew. She nodded her understanding. "Although that doesn't say much about your opinion of the wedded state. No matter, you've only given me what a mistress must not do, which is no help in knowing what I should do."

Courtney was wondering if he could come out and say a mistress should be adoring, alluring, and provocative. Not while Miss Partland had a raspberry ice in her hand, he decided. He also wondered if Miss Partland had any passion whatsoever in her governess's soul. "Oh, just be yourself," he concluded, hoping for the best.

Taking it for a compliment, Kathlyn smiled up at him in

as doting a fashion as he could have wished, the raspberries making her lips seem that they'd just been kissed. Oh yes.

Gorblimey, who read all this claptrap? What did anyone care which duke was sniffing after what baronet's wife or how long some general had been away from his lady and her interesting condition? Inspector Dimm closed the newspaper with a snap. Interesting, pah! Mr. Dimm found it disgusting. Didn't any of these toffs keep their vows? His own wife, Cora, God bless her and keep her, would have had his guts for garters if he looked at another woman. He never was unfaithful, by George, not in all the years of his marriage, and hadn't been unfaithful to Cora's memory since she went to her reward.

But Cora'd been gone awhile, and, well, a fellow got lonely now and again. He wanted to feel something soft and small and warm and cuddlesome, something other than his cat. Maybe the nobs had the right idea, taking pleasure where they found it. And maybe Miss Partland just got to feeling lonely after her pa died. She wasn't coming to the park today either, so Dimm decided he may as well go on home, to his empty, echoing house. He also decided that he'd ask that nice widow lady, the dark-haired one who came veiled to the park every day to feed the squirrels and who took such an interest in his work, if she wanted to share a hackney. Dimm didn't like seeing women out on their own without escorts. London was too rough for the delicate dears.

Chapter Ten

$\mathcal{A}$ thousand suns were shining at the Opera House, what joy! The candles, the chandeliers, the gem-studded audience, Kathlyn was entranced by it all, even if this was merely a benefit night. The Opera House would not open officially until April when the social season began for the upper crust, but Kathlyn's official debut as a rich man's tart would occur this evening.

Lord Chase had decided that Kitty needed a bit of exposure to the public eye before the Cyprians' Ball, especially after she confessed to never having attended an assembly of more than a hundred people back in Cheshire. She'd known most of her dance partners there, the neighboring tenant farmers and tradesmen, for her entire life. The local gentry rarely deigned to appear at such provincial gatherings, for which the commoners gave thanks and another shilling to the fiddler to play another country dance. Nothing in Kathlyn's life as the dowerless daughter of an impecunious Latin instructor could have prepared her for this night. She was going to get a crick in her neck from swiveling it, trying to see everything—and the curtain hadn't even been raised yet. If others, especially the young bucks in the pit, were standing on the benches trying to get a good look at her

78

in his lordship's box, Kathlyn didn't care. She felt like a princess tonight.

Her spirits had never been higher, and her neckline had never been lower. Nanny and Lizzie both assured her that ladies of the ton had their bodices cut still narrower. No one ever mentioned what ladies of the night wore, and Kathlyn didn't inquire. Her gown was something a fairy godmother might have conjured out of cobwebs and moonbeams, a slip dress of silver silk with a midnight blue net overskirt. She had long silver gloves and silver sandals, and a coronet of white roses holding her hair, except for the long black curl twining over her shoulder.

Kitty mightn't be offended by the ogles and whistles from the pit and the other boxes, but Courtney was and he resented them on her behalf, since she appeared too excited to notice. It was what he wanted, of course, for his companion to be admired, but those loudmouthed boors were going beyond the line. Not that Courtney could blame them, he could barely keep his eyes off her himself, so stunning was his little snow waif. Hah! She was the most beautiful female here this evening, and she was with him. He touched that silken curl on her shoulder—which he'd been longing to do all night—to stake his claim. He left his arm draped across the back of her chair. Kathlyn just turned and smiled. "Isn't it exciting, my lord?"

If she only knew . . .

Courtney turned his attention to the other boxes, and grew more annoyed when he saw all the lorgnettes and quizzing glasses aimed in their direction. 'Twould seem that his lordship needed more getting used to public scrutiny than Kitty did. Deuce take it, though, every pair of opera glasses meant another letter to his mother in Trowbridge. That was inevitable. Courtney was surprised he hadn't heard from Lady Chase already, after her coterie of spies informed her he was squiring a Diamond about Town this week.

Which reminded him, blast, that Kitty should have

jewels at her throat, dangling from her ears, and encircling her slender wrist.

"No, my lord," she'd firmly stated. "I shall not accept jewelry from you. The clothes are a necessary adjunct to our pretense, and the salary, of course, is part of the bargain. Jewels are not."

"Would you accept a loan?"

"What, your family heirlooms? Now that would put the cat among the pigeons, my lord."

And have his mother back from Trowbridge before the last snowflake melted. Still, he wasn't pleased. "It will make me look like a nip-cheese."

"Diamonds will make me look like a whore."

So Courtney relented, pleased that under all the sweetness, Miss Partland still had backbone. She would need it to face the world.

No, he thought, she needed her cloak, for Nanny had been right, Miss Kathlyn did not require a diamond to set off her looks. The purity of her skin, the rise of her breasts above the neckline, the sharp valley between them, drew a man's eye like no jewel ever could. Blast, Courtney wished she had on her brown sack dress, buttoned to the neck.

There was a young Tulip in yellow pantaloons in the pit who, raised on his equally castaway friends' shoulders, began tossing roses in Kitty's direction. Soon all the striplings in the cheap seats were throwing flowers and their calling cards at the viscount's box, loudly begging for a smile, her name, her address. They all missed, to everyone's hilarity but Courtney's. He raised her gloved hand to his lips, in plain sight. "Ignore them," the viscount told her.

"Of course, my lord, they're only boys with high spirits. They mean nothing by their antics."

Not even a schoolmistress from Cheshire could be that unaware. Courtney groaned and drew his chair closer to hers, then placed his arm on her shoulder, so her side was pressed against his.

Kathlyn looked up, startled. "My lord?"

He leaned even closer, whispering in her ear in a loverlike manner. "Mine," was all he said.

Kathlyn laughed. Of course. He was acting the smitten beau. And he was very good at it.

Her laughter pleased him. It wasn't the giggle or twitter that passed for humor among the debutante set, nor the restrained simper of an older woman, just sheer, sweet happiness. She should laugh like that for the rest of her life. Remembering the pinch-faced, sour-visaged, acid-tongued hag whom he'd rescued from the snow, Courtney vowed she'd never be anyone's drudge again. He'd give her a marriage portion if he could, but that would never do. His dowering an unrelated female was bound to come out, then where would she be? On the streets for real. Besides, the clerks and farmers she was like to wed were too far beneath her. Wealthy merchants only wanted titled daughters of the aristocracy for their sons, so their grand-children could be accepted where they themselves never were.

No, Miss Partland would do better with that school of her own, he thought, not acknowledging how relieved he was to eliminate a husband from Kitty's future. She was wonderful with Nanny's grandchildren, and had even begun teaching Lizzie to read. Nanny adored her, and he himself found her intelligent and capable and steady. Kitty was a good sport, too, taking the catcalls and the ogling better than he was, ignoring them in favor of the glittering surroundings. Courtney was praying for the blasted opera to begin. A strong-lunged, love-stricken soprano never held more appeal.

At the first intermission, Courtney escorted Kitty out of their box and down the corridor to get some air and a lemonade. Scores of young gentlemen lined the hall and the stairs, waiting for just such an opportunity to meet Chase's new dasher. Rather than stop to talk to the rattlepates, Courtney held Kitty close by his side and whispered to her—about the opera, but the loiterers were not to know that. As the viscount planned, they thought he was whispering sweet words of love. He intercepted smirks, winks, and a few fingers laid alongside noses.

A handful of acquaintances were too determined to be introduced for Chase to ignore. When one of these old school chums or former fellow officers planted himself in their path, Courtney had no option but to present his companion, Miss Kitty Parke. He held her hand in his, though, so none of the bounders could play the gallant by slobbering over it. Then he quickly hurried her away, claiming a burning thirst, before the lascivious lowlifes could shower Kitty with Spanish coin or personal questions. That heavy-handed flattery could only be embarrassing for a girl not used to it, and any inquiry more pointed than her opinion of the opera was an invasion of her privacy, too dangerous to their masquerade, and a scoundrel's strategy.

Courtney knew how these basket-scramblers operated: they showed interest in the latest comet, disdaining the female on their arm. They feigned fascination with the new dazzler's person, swearing entrancement by her beauty, when all they wanted was to pry her away from her current protector. The man with the most desirable mistress, the man whose mistress was desired by the most men, rather, was considered a hero in this benighted society. To them it was all a game. Well, Kitty was no pawn. She was under contract to him, by Jupiter. And when Courtney was done playacting his rake's role, she was *not* going to be handed around from man to man like a horse on the block at Tattersall's. He wasn't sacrificing her virtue to protect his own.

On the other hand, a chap didn't call out a close friend for staring at his mistress's bosom. Hell and damnation! Courtney gulped down his lemonade, then rushed Kitty back to their seats in his blessedly empty box.

* * *

At the next intermission, Courtney was determined to stay in the box, even should Kitty profess a parched throat. Then Algie came to visit. How could the viscount tell his oldest friend to go to the devil?

Lord Algernon Lowe wouldn't have listened anyway, he was too busy pumping Kathlyn's hand up and down, slapping Courtney on the back, and grinning. "I knew you wouldn't let the home team down, old man. Wagered Woodbury a pony on it, I did. But you sly dog, you, keeping such a treasure under wraps. Can't blame you, of course. The foxes are already slavering at the henhouse, heh heh."

Before Algie could embarrass them all any further, Courtney asked, "Is Woodbury with you?" Algie and Vernon Woodbury, Bart., were nearly inseparable members of the Corinthian set.

Algie took his eyes off Kathlyn barely long enough to answer. "No, I'm here with the family, more's the pity. Woody ain't in the petticoat line." Noting Kathlyn's confusion, Algie pointed to a nearby box where three women sat, two girls in white gowns and an older lady in puce, with a magenta turban sporting two ostrich feathers. "Five sisters, don't you know."

"Good grief, Algie, how did you get escort duty?" Lord Lowe was more often found on the hunting field than on the dance floor.

"Pater stayed on in Kent to oversee some improvements." He grimaced. "Promised to be here for the Season so I won't have to do the pretty at all those balls and things. Mama and the girls came early to get a start on their shopping. Have to get a jump on the other debs, don't you know."

"Which sister is being brought out this year?"

"The middle two. Mama decided to fire 'em off together and get it over with. Where she hopes to find two gudgeons to bring up to scratch is beyond me."

Kathlyn smiled at the tall, thin man dressed to the

nines—but not as elegantly as Lord Chase. "I am sure they are delightful girls, Lord Lowe."

He nodded approvingly. "And I'm sure you are too polite to say otherwise, Miss Parke. Stands to reason old Court wouldn't be squiring an antidote and wouldn't be taking a common trollop to his b— Ouch."

"Your sisters?" Lord Chase hinted while Algie rubbed his shin.

"Two of the silliest geese ever let off the farm, I swear, Miss Parke. One's a hoyden, t'other's a flirt. Ain't that true, Court? You haven't seen them in a while, but I promise they ain't improved with age."

"I'm sure they've grown out of their freckles and foibles, Algie. They cannot be any sillier than the rest of the chits at Almack's."

"And I'm sure they aren't silly at all, my lord," Kathlyn chided, "only young. I'd like to meet them." Silence met her last remark. Algie's face grew red, then white. His mouth opened and shut like a trout's, out of water. Lord Chase cleared his throat, then checked his watch. "Intermission's about over, Algie. Time you toddled back to your seat."

Kathlyn knew she'd said something dreadful to halt the pleasantries, but she didn't know what until she repeated her last comments in her own mind. Of course. A man didn't introduce a courtesan to his young, impressionable sisters; immoral behavior might be contagious. Scarlet-faced, Kathlyn stuttered, "I . . . I meant I should like to meet their . . . their modiste. Their gowns look quite elegant."

A relieved Algie swept her a handsome leg and departed.

When he was gone, Kathlyn made much of unfolding her fan and wafting it about. The fan was a pretty affair of blue silk over ivory spokes, with a pair of picnicking lovers depicted on one side. It did not create enough of a breeze to cool her burning cheeks.

"I'm sorry," she finally managed to say. "I should have known better."

84

"No, the fault was mine." He took the fan from her and gently waved it, meanwhile stroking her almost bare shoulder. "I should have warned you. The ton has a thousand foolish edicts handed down by old harridans who did much worse in their lifetimes. I never thought about such situations, Miss— Kitty, because I do not think of you in those terms."

Of course he didn't, but everyone else did, it seemed. "They all know I'm your . . . That is, I'm supposed to be your mistress?"

He shrugged. "You have no chaperone. There is no other lady in the box. We arrived alone in my carriage. That's enough for the social world to draw conclusions."

"Conclusions which we were aiming to encourage, weren't we?" she asked brightly, so he could not see her hurt.

Courtney was feeling regrets, too, though, for he brought her hand to his mouth and kissed her fingers. "On the inside, you are more a lady than any of them. That's what's important."

Chapter Eleven

"*N*ot more snow?" Snowflakes were settling on Kathlyn's cloak while she and Courtney waited outside the opera for their carriage to be brought 'round. "I so wanted to see the new steam engine tomorrow."

"Perhaps this is only a flurry. Let's stand there, under the overhang."

Others had the same idea. Soon quite a crowd was pressed into the narrow protected area. Of the happy theater-goers, some gentlemen were made known to Kathlyn, others not. Of the ones Courtney did present, he also introduced some of their female companions, some not. Of the women, Kathlyn was beginning to note the difference in the ones whose names Lord Chase gave: the harsher look, the coarser accents, the first-name familiarity, and a bit of face paint here and there streaking in the wet falling snow. More definitively, the hired ladies wore more jewelry than the "real" ladies. Kathlyn's bare throat pleased her better than any of the gaudy necklaces she saw.

A gentleman with his arm around a red-haired girl invited the viscount and Kitty to join them at the Pulteney for a late supper. Two others seconded the invite.

Courtney had been planning on taking Kitty there for dinner, telling himself they had to plan their costumes for the Cyprians' Ball. Mainly he hadn't tired of looking at her yet. Now he couldn't take her there, not to have her by himself, without seeming standoffish. And the evening had been harrowing enough, what with every lecher trying to see through Kitty's gown. The ball was unavoidable, but Courtney had never meant to expose his misplaced governess to more vulgarity than necessary. The language at these late dinners could become quite warm, not meant for tender ears, and the behavior rowdier still, especially if a private parlor was hired.

"Sorry," he said, "we have other plans." It might have been better to accept, then go on their way after a toast or two, before the party grew uninhibited. Now he had to put up with loud guffaws and ribald comments about those "other plans." Thank goodness, Courtney thought, Kitty wouldn't understand the half of them.

The boisterous, cheerful crowd moved off, settling into two carriages, the females atop the men's laps so they'd all fit.

"Shameless," declared a woman behind Courtney.

He turned to see which old harridan was so offended. Surprisingly, it wasn't one of his mother's cronies at all. "Lady Fostwick, my lord." Courtney made a polite bow and turned back.

Lady Fostwick, née Adelina Marlowe, wasn't letting the viscount off that easily. She jerked her head in Kathlyn's direction, snapping an egret feather from her headpiece into her husband's left eye. "I see your lofty principles barely lasted as long as the engagement, sirrah," she sniped.

Courtney bent his head in her husband's direction. "And I see your heartbreak lasted almost until the next Venetian breakfast, my lady."

Refusing to let Courtney think she still pined for his golden curls, dimpled cheeks, or forty thousand a year, Adelina tittered. "La, sir, heartbreak? What did hearts ever have to do with such arrangements?"

"What, indeed?" Lord Chase glanced at Fostwick, Adelina's senior by at least thirty years, in his old-fashioned bag wig, with snuff stains dribbled down his shirtfront. "My belated congratulations, my lord. Excuse me for not offering them sooner, but I was on the Peninsula. Word of your marriage did not arrive until too many months were passed."

"Quite, quite. Lucky man, eh?"

Adelina had chipmunk cheeks, two chins, and sausage-shaped fingers. "Indeed, but not as fortunate as I consider myself," Courtney declared. Before Adelina could interpret that barbed comment correctly, the viscount drew Kathlyn forward. "My dear, may I present Lord and Lady Fostwick. Miss Kitty Parke."

Bright spots of color appeared on Adelina's plump cheeks. She bobbed her head a scant quarter of an inch, then grabbed Fostwick's arm. "Let us wait inside, Fostwick. The air is too insalubrious here."

"Quite, quite." As the couple moved away, Courtney and Kathlyn could hear Lord Fostwick muttering, "Should have presented the chit to you, a married lady and a baroness. Not t'other way around, a plain miss years younger. Ouch, that was my gouty toe you tripped on, ma'am. Stap me if this new generation ain't too casual about such things."

"Shut up, you old bladder of wind. Chase shouldn't have introduced me to her at all. The jade is his paramour!"

"Fortunate devil. Ouch. Do watch your step, my pet. But you are quite right, he should not have presented the female. Not at all the thing. Grievous insult, I believe. I shall have to call him out first thing in the morning."

Adelina looked over her shoulder to note Courtney's

broad back and muscular legs despite the limp. Then she looked at her hunched-over, chicken-breasted husband. His eyesight was so poor, he couldn't see Lord Chase at twenty paces, and his hand shook so badly, he'd never hit him if he did. Then his son by his first marriage would inherit and Adelina would have nothing but her widow's portion. "Don't be an ass, Fostwick."

After Lord Chase handed Kathlyn into the crested coach and tucked the rug around her knees, he took the seat next to her, rather than the facing one. "In case anyone is watching," he explained, since they'd had to take the closed carriage on such a chill night. The driver and footman might be loyal, but they might also be loquacious.

Kathlyn didn't mind the viscount's closeness, welcoming the warmth and savoring the lemony scent of his cologne. She did mind the confusing scene back at the Opera House. "That woman, Lady Fostwick, wasn't a courtesan at all, was she?"

Chase stretched his wounded leg out more comfortably. "Not precisely. She was my former fiancée."

"But what about those strictures of society? You should not have introduced us."

"You're right, and I apologize profoundly for any discomfort the introduction may have caused you."

Now Kathlyn was more confused. "You're apologizing . . . to me?"

He was absently stroking her fingers in his hand, ostensibly to warm them. "Adelina Marlowe, Lady Fostwick, deserves the husband she got. She isn't fit to touch your hem, Kitty."

His words did more to warm her than his touch, but that was lovely, too. Kathlyn had to smile at the thought of that haughty society matron being considered soiled goods. "Next you'll be telling me I'm too good for royalty."

"Deuced right you are. Our royal dukes are the most worthless libertines in Britain, and Prinny himself would be the last man I'd want you near. He's the worst of the lot, for besides having excellent taste, he's dashed hard to refuse. Recently, of course, he's been fascinated with older women, but he still has an eye for a pretty face. No, I pray you never come to his attention. I'd have to emigrate to the Americas for refusing to make the introduction."

She had to laugh. "What fustian. Why would you care if I met the prince?"

And was despoiled by His Royally Lecherous Highness, why indeed? Why should he care if Kitty heard lewd suggestions, received indecent proposals, saw the aristocracy in rut? She was no milk-and-water miss, nor was she his responsibility. Without family, money, or education, many of her sisters had no choice but to take the primrose path. They'd be happy if Courtney set their feet in the right direction. Not Miss Partland. Never Miss Partland, he swore, for no good reason that he wished to examine or discuss. "Why would I keep you out of Prinny's plump clutches? My investment, don't you know."

Ah. Kathlyn pulled her hand away to tidy an errant curl. Then she stared out at the swirling flakes. Lord Chase was right, it was only a flurry. And she was only an investment.

Good, Kathlyn thought, she'd needed the reminder. A few days and nights in the viscount's company, with his lordship on his best behavior because he needed her cooperation, almost let her forget what an arrogant, self-righteous prig his lordship could be. She wasn't good enough for him, and he wasn't ever in danger of forgetting that.

Well, he wasn't good enough for her either. He might be the finest gentleman she was ever likely to meet, appearing to offer everything a girl could want out of life. But appearances were deceptive, she recalled. She wasn't a prostitute, and he couldn't use one.

Lord Chase was handsome and rich, intelligent and kind to his dependents, but Kathlyn didn't need a big house and balls every night. She wanted a little home of her own, a loving husband, and a family, the one thing his lordship could not provide. Let him find that woman who'd be content to bear his illustrious name, without bearing his children.

As always, the thought of the viscount's vicissitudes made Kathlyn relent, pitying the poor man for his grievous loss. So when he kissed her good night outside Nanny's, for the coachmen's benefit, she went gladly into his arms. He could mean nothing but pretense and platonic affection by it, Kathlyn told herself, so she might as well discover what kissing was about while she had the chance before setting up her school.

Miss Partland had been smacked on the lips by Squire's son one afternoon after his lessons with her father. She'd taught him another lesson, blackening his eye for him. But this was nothing at all like that. There was nothing furtive or frenzied in the viscount's kiss; it simply felt nice, all tingly, with snowflakes on his lips. Very nice, very nonthreatening because Kathlyn knew he wasn't going to maul her about or ask for more than she was willing to give. Exceptionally nice. By the time his lordship was done with the pretend kiss, the just-for-show kiss, Kathlyn's knees were like jelly, and she couldn't feel her toes at all. No, she felt her toes, but not the ground they stood upon. The poor man must have been a wonderful lover before his injury.

The poor man dismissed the carriage before he could order it to Harriet Wilson's place. He'd walk home, despite his injury.

* * *

"Aha! That's got to be my pigeon, gorblimey!"

"What's that, dear Mr. Dimm? I thought you liked the sweet little squirrels best, not the pigeons." Ursula Miner frowned at the sack of nuts in her hand, the fourth sack of nuts this week. She was no closer to finding her jewels or the female who had them than those rubbishing rodents. Her only consolation was that neither was Quigley, who was skulking in the bushes still, nor Bow Street's doddering detective. Neither one had recognized Harry's widow in her wig and veil, but neither one had found Harry's haul either.

Inspector Dimm folded the newspaper to the gossip page, delighted that he could get his butt off the cold bench at last. "Here, listen to this: 'The polite world was agog last night to see a certain hero of the Peninsula sharing his opera box with an unknown Diamond. The raven-haired beauty did not seem to be giving much of a chase to our courting viscount.' That's got to be her, b'gad."

"Her?" Ursula asked, showing polite interest instead of going for the old man's throat. Four days of feeding scurvy squirrels and cozying up to Father Time, and the thief-taker had bought her one cup of tea, one hackney ride, and the information that they were looking for a new ladybird recently taken under some gent's wing. And all of those bushy-tailed vermin were begging at her feet. "The female you were looking for?"

"Aye. Now I know for sure that she's still in Town."

"But do you know where to locate her?" Ursula wasn't sure Dimm knew where to locate his trouser flap, he'd been so cold to her overtures. She'd even had to rent an apartment, thanks to the cheap old codger.

"Someone at Bow Street's bound to know which viscount. These here *on dits* columns, that's what they call the tripe, give clues and hints. Should be easy enough to find where he keeps his sweethearts stashed. No matter, the young buck'll be bringing his sweetie to the Cyprians' Ball in a few days. I'll get Nipperkin back. We'll spot her there."

"The, ah, Cyprians' Ball, you say? My, I haven't been to a ball in ever so long. . . ."

"My apologies, ma'am, I shouldn't have mentioned it. Not for a lady's ears. And I'll be on duty, a' course."

"Of course. So conscientious."

"Right, that's how I get the job done. Be leaving now, I will, off to report to the governor. Been a pleasure, ma'am, and I hope you'll share my bag of nuts here another day."

"Oh yes, it's my favorite thing above all." Ursula waited till Dimm's back was turned, then kicked at a squirrel near her booted foot. "Pesky park rats."

Quigley was so hungry, he was thinking of snaring one of those ratty-looking squirrels the widow woman was always feeding—or stealing one of the nuts. It would be the only thing he managed to steal this week.

Quigley didn't have a shilling to his name, wasn't a good footpad, and was about to lose his lodgings at Shippy's, where there'd been no news from Sean but plenty of lice and bedbugs.

He didn't know what else to do except watch the old gaffer act the mooncalf for some veiled mutton done up as lamb. Every morning he trailed Dimm from Bow Street to the park, hiding in the bushes, trying not to scratch himself. Then he followed the Runner back to Bow Street after all the nobs had ridden through Rotten Row. Quigley thought he could rob a bank if this was the best Bow Street could do.

Maybe when Sean came back they'd go into that line of work. They'd held up that coach all right and tight, too, even if they hadn't thought to take anything. Maybe they could be highwaymen. They sure as hell couldn't be cracksmen again, not without Harry.

It was Harry who always planned their jobs, Harry who fenced the jewelry, and Harry who divided the money. Damn, Quigley missed old Harry. Wished they hadn't of killed him, too, leastways till they knew where the diamonds were. Wished he didn't have flea bites on his rump.

Chapter Twelve

$\mathcal{A}$nother storm was raging, but this one was in Nanny Dawson's front parlor. Lord Chase was holding out for the harem costume for the ball, bare midriff, gauze pantaloons, and a gem in Kitty's navel.

Nanny was having none of it. "Not even over my dead body, Master Courtney, for I'd come back to haunt you from the grave if you dressed our Miss Kitty in anything so wicked."

Kathlyn wanted to wear her lovely evening gown, with stars and moons sewn on the midnight blue overdress and a feathered mask like the one she'd seen at the milliner's. "A mysterious lady of the night. Quite fitting, I think, my lord."

"What, and hide half your face? I think not."

Lizzie thought her lady should wear a gray domino with little pointed ears sewn on the hood and whiskers painted on her cheeks. Dressing Kitty as a cat was considered a charming notion, but not quite what his lordship had in mind. Courtney wanted something beautiful, somewhat risqué, and certainly memorable. After that night, no one was to doubt his taste or his virility. They dressed her as a Gypsy, and he got his wish.

Kathlyn wore her hair loose down her back, held off

her face with two Spanish combs Courtney'd brought home from the Peninsula, a red rose tucked in one of them. Her hair fell in silky waves past her waist, which was cinched to hand-span width despite Nanny's rich cooking. She wore a rose-embroidered, white peasant blouse on top, loose enough to fall suggestively over her shoulders, low enough to show the top of her lace chemise—and a great deal of soft white skin. Below, her skirt was black, held out by six swirling red petticoats, showing off her neat ankles and dainty black slippers. Courtney was all for having her go barefoot, but was overridden again.

"What, in this weather? She'll take a chill and die afore morning."

"His lordship won't care, so long as he gets his money's worth tonight." Kathlyn was growing nervous about the coming ordeal and aggravated that the viscount was looking at her like a piece of merchandise he was considering purchasing. Heaven knew he'd already made his bargain.

The outfit was deemed complete with gold hoops in her ears, coins around her neck, and bangles jingling at her wrists. Kathlyn loved the noise, the swish of satin petticoats and the tinkle of the coins; she adored the freedom of loose skirts and unbound hair. Twirling in front of the mirror in her room, Kathlyn thought she could envy the Gypsies, the Gypsies in fairy tales, anyway, for she didn't think she'd like sleeping in a wagon or eating rabbit stew by a campfire and never having a hot bath. Well, she was a lady pretending to be a courtesan who was pretending to be a Gypsy; she might as well pretend a better life for her character, Madame Katerina Paki. And she couldn't have imagined a better partner for 'Madame Paki.' There might not be many blond, blue-eyed Gypsy Roms, but for 'Katerina,' Lord Chase was the only match. The viscount wore tight black breeches tucked into high boots, and a loose white shirt with billowing sleeves. Kathlyn tried not to notice the golden mat of hair that followed the open shirt to his red sash.

Nanny thought the gold hoop in one ear made his lordship look more like a pirate than a Gypsy. Kathlyn thought it wouldn't matter. He could steal any number of hearts, whatever guise he wore. Thank goodness her knowledge of him kept her safe from such temptation, she told herself, peeking once more at the bronzed muscles his shirt left uncovered. Oh, dear, yes.

For Courtney's sake all that mattered was that their costumes matched. He tucked a red rose in his sash, a twin to the one Kitty wore in her hair. He was willing to let the loose screws see her beauty, her sheer feminine desirability—as long as they saw that she was his.

Their reception at the Argyle Rooms was everything Lord Chase had wanted, and more. Too much more. Too many men wanted to dance with Madame Katerina or bring her champagne—hell, Courtney thought, they wanted to lick her toes! Thank goodness she wasn't barefoot after all. If they held an auction for her favors this very night, Kitty would have enough blunt to open her school tomorrow. Deuce take it, he swore, she'd have enough to open a bloody university.

Every dirty dish in London was panting at her skirts, like a pack of foxhounds with their tongues hanging out. Blast, why couldn't they find their own light-o'-loves for the evening and leave his alone! He couldn't get her away by dancing with her, not with his bad leg, and it was too soon to leave. Then he saw his friends Algie and Woody. The very thing.

After the greetings and Kitty's introduction to Sir Vernon Woodbury, Bart., Courtney begged a favor. "I don't like Kitty being importuned by these rotters. I need you two to help shield her from the wilder elements. You know, dance with her, stand around making conversation, not let her get dragged off to waltz with any castaway court-cards."

Algie volunteered immediately. "No hardship, I assure you, old man." He was a little too eager, earning a frown from Lord Chase, so he added, "Don't get in a fidge, Court, you know I wouldn't poach in your preserves. I'll guard Miss Kitty as carefully as one of m'own sisters." No, Algie didn't want to mention sisters again. "Better, I'll treat her like a china doll, that's it."

Swept off into her very first waltz, Kathlyn looked back toward the viscount, who was left standing with a roistering group of men in togas, tights, and more typical evening wear. Lord Chase was the most dashing by far. She'd much rather be in his arms this very minute, swaying to the rhythms of the music, but he couldn't waltz. He couldn't— She let the thought die. "How tragic it is about his lordship's wound."

"Old Courtney? He'll get over it."

Get over it, she wondered, like a sprained ankle? Or perhaps Algie didn't know. "But it keeps him from so many things," she hinted. "Like dancing."

"He did used to dance, now I think on it, but old Court always had devilish odd notions about women, even before the war. Too particular by half. Can't tell you how happy I am to see you, miss."

As they took their places for the next set, Sir Vernon, Woody to everyone, proved to be no more help to Kathlyn in understanding the viscount than Algie had been. He merely grinned his schoolboyish smile and held his hand over his heart, so it didn't fall out of his chest at her feet. After the dance he escorted her back to the viscount. "Sorry, Court, I'll be no help defending your lady. Want to carry her off m'self, don't you know. And I ain't in the petticoat line any more than you were. She's irresistible, that's all."

"Thunderation, you clothhead, can't you see you're putting Kitty to the blush?" They were all watching the blush rise from her décolletage. "Blast, if I can't trust my best friends with her, we better go home."

"Not so soon," begged Woody, pale eyes popping out of his head.

Algie put in, "Not everyone's here yet, Court. You've got to stay and let them all drown in their envy." Algie had money on Courtney's bringing the handsomest female to the ball, to be decided at the midnight unmasking. Algie wasn't about to confess that to Chase, not with the viscount looking thunderclouds already. Courtney fell hard, when he finally fell. Too bad it was over a ladybird. "Stop acting like a hen with one chick or people are going to get the wrong idea. People like your mother," he warned in a loud whisper.

Meanwhile, Woody had been thinking of a way to keep this goddess at the ball where he could worship her at a short distance—the length of Chase's sword. "I have it, Court. Let her tell fortunes. We'll pull some chairs together, screen her off a bit, then let one or two females at a time come by for her to tell if they're going to marry tall, dark strangers."

"The fortune-teller's is the first tent m'sisters visit at every fair." Damn, there Algie was, mentioning his siblings again to a demirep. "Well, females here can't be any sillier. And you might earn a few pennies, too, Miss Kitty, 'cause you're supposed to cross a Gypsy's hand with silver for a reading."

Kathlyn was thinking what nice gentlemen these two addlepates were to concern themselves with protecting their friend's inamorata from the rougher elements of such a gathering. Surely they had to know of his handicap, then, to think him not man enough to defend his property. Laughing at their method of assistance, Kathlyn said, "Gammon, my lords. I cannot tell fortunes. I never even heard one because my father thought it all pagan superstition. Besides, we have no crystal ball."

"You don't need one. The old hags m'sisters consult just look at their hands. See this line here on my palm? That means long life. After you say that, you can promise 'em whatever they want to hear."

Woody added, "Only don't tell the females here they'll have a parcel of brats. Bad for business, don't you know."

Courtney was smiling. "That sounds like a fine idea to me. Here, start with me." He held out his hand.

It must be the champagne, Kathlyn decided, for she couldn't think of her name, much less his fortune. She shook herself. Kathlyn. No, Kitty. No, she was Katerina tonight, and her trembling hand might hold his, but Courtney's future did not hold her. Kathlyn didn't need any tea leaves to know that.

They were all waiting, so she said, "Whatever your heart most desires is within your grasp. You only have to recognize it."

"That's the ticket," Algie congratulated. "General, with a hint of mystery. The more obscure the better. Now try Woody's."

"I don't care about m'future," the baronet confided, "if I get to hold a pretty gel's hand." They all laughed—except Courtney—so Woody told Kitty, "I don't want to hear about legshackles and offspring, either. No need to get a fellow depressed. But I'm devilish anxious to know who'll win the speed trials at Epsom next week."

Kathlyn smiled. "I don't even know who's running, Sir Vernon. I'm sorry, I'm not very good at this."

Algie urged her on. "Nonsense, you've got women's intuition and all that. Just think."

So she thought, then finally said, "Well, the fastest horse will win, and the one with the most luck. That's all my intuition tells me. I'm sorry it's not more profound."

Woody wrote it down while the others sipped their champagne. "Do you see any silks, Miss Kitty? Colors?"

She was still seeing the golden hairs on Lord Chase's chest taper into the red sash. "Gold," she said. "Gold and scarlet."

Woody kept writing. "Couldn't be a worse system than the one I've been using."

When it was Algie's turn, Kathlyn told him, "I see an older gentleman and green fields and, yes, sheep."

"By George, she does have the knack! The pater wrote that he's delayed in Kent overseeing repairs to the sheep pens after the heavy snows! Deuce take it, Courtney, how'd you find a female as talented as she is beautiful?"

"You might say she fell from the sky, like an angel, or a snowflake."

And so Kathlyn sat smiling through ninety minutes of the Cyprians' Ball, his lordship's hand on her shoulder, Algie and Woody flanking her. She told fortunes to the frail sisterhood, mixing in French and her smattering of German to sound more authentic and more arcane. Trying not to give false hopes by predicting anything too far-fetched, Kathlyn, Madame Katerina, promised the ladies great riches, a handsome gentleman, a trip in an elegant carriage, a shiny trinket.

"Do you see any diamonds, madam?" one bottle blonde in a shepherdess's costume wanted to know. "A necklace with a stone the size of a pigeon's egg set in a crown of rubies, and diamond and ruby earbobs that hang to your shoulders."

Oh dear, that was a high order. The woman must really want them, she was staring at Kathlyn so intently, but the tall shepherd with her didn't seem prosperous enough. Wearing a hooded weskit that must be itchy, he seemed more interested in food than the tightly laced blonde. Kathlyn didn't want to lie to the poor woman, who must have seen such a set of jewels in some Bond Street window. It would be cruel to lead her on that way. "No, but I do think I see something else around your neck. Something . . ."

"Are you sure? Sure you ain't never seen anything like that recently?"

This telling fortunes was an odd business, but Kathlyn had to laugh. "Oh, I'm sure I'd remember seeing a necklace like that, in your future or mine! I'm certain neither of us would be here if we owned such a treasure."

"I'll drink to that, ducks."

* * *

"She ain't got it," Harry's widow told Quigley. Ursula had decided to bring him along in case the female was wearing Harry's jewels, so the thug could help waylay the handsome swell the mort was with. That was too bad. Ursula wouldn't mind some time with the gentry cove herself, after they got the sparklers back. She didn't think he'd look at her with his Gypsy around, though; the out-and-outer wasn't noticing any of the other half-naked females waggling their wares in front of him. Crossing the viscount off her list of possibilities, Ursula figured she might as well see about finding herself a new protector while she was here, since the jewels weren't.

She got rid of Quigley easily enough, sending him and his crooked staff in the direction of the refreshments room, then she looked around. But damn, Ursula Miner hated the idea of earning jewelry the old way.

Inspector Dimm was outside in the cold. He knew now which viscount that article had meant, knew which carriage belonged to Lord Chase, and knew his quarry would be easy to identify when they left the ball. He had a hackney all ready to follow them, so he chewed on his pipe, tried to keep his feet out of the puddles, and watched the front door.

"What a disguise!" Dimm had seen a lot of disguises in his line of work, but tonight he was impressed. "The woman must be some kind of mastermind."

"What, the Gypsy whore?" Ripken asked.

"No, you clunch, the spinster schoolteacher."

Chapter Thirteen

"*But* it's bitter out, and there is ice on the streets. You cannot walk home in this, not with your bad leg."

"Hush, Kitty." The viscount held her to his side, his arm at her waist, as they walked up the little path to Nanny's. He moved his head to indicate the driver turning the coach. "There'd be talk if I didn't spend the night. I'll see you inside, stay a few minutes, and then leave. Not even Nanny can find impropriety in that, but it will satisfy the gabble-grinders if my driver or the footman mentions where they've been. I can hire a hackney to take me home afterward if my leg is bothering me."

Once inside, Kathlyn lit the parlor candles, hung her cloak on a peg, and fussed with the banked fireplace coals. Anything to avoid watching him walk out of her life.

Courtney was leaning against the windowsill, smiling at her nervousness. "Goose, don't you know by now that you can trust me?"

"Of course. It's not that, but . . ."

"But it's over, right?"

"That was our bargain." Kathlyn was fingering the bracelets at her wrists.

"And we succeeded tonight, didn't we? Beyond my wildest expectations. Everyone loved you!"

"And it was fun, telling fortunes that way. I liked it much better than if I'd had to make conversation with all those strangers."

"No one offended you, did they?"

"Of course not, not with you growling like a bear over my shoulder all evening."

Courtney removed the gold hoop from his ear and pretended to study it. "I, ah, realize some of the public displays at an event like that are not for tender sensibilities."

"Oh, no, you and your friends kept anything untoward out of my sight." Three large males standing so close blocked almost everything.

"Yes, well, I don't want you to think that all men hold women so cheaply, even at a marketplace such as tonight."

"No, Algie and Woody and yourself, of course, my lord, were perfect gentlemen."

He nodded, satisfied, and took a bank draft out of his pocket. "That's it, then. Our business is concluded. But," he hurried on when she came over to accept the check, "but you mustn't think you have to rush off right away. Nanny would love you to stay on, at least until her Meg has the baby, and we never did get to view the waxworks. Besides, no trip to London can be complete without a visit to Astley's Amphitheatre to see the equestrian acts. We could even take Meg's children along, as an excuse for pursuing such juvenile entertainment. What do you think?"

Kathlyn thought that sounded heavenly, except that she had her way to make in the world. The longer she stayed in such comfortable surroundings, the harder it would be to leave. And the harder it would be to leave his lordship. She started to shake her head.

"No, no, don't refuse out of hand. Think about it, and listen to Nanny's pleas in the morning. If it's the money you're worried about, you won't have a ha'penny's expense, you know, for the mortgage here is all paid, and the coal and such is my responsibility. You don't eat more than a bird, so that won't bankrupt anyone either."

"Very well, I'll think on it, and ask Nanny's advice about starting a school here in London."

After attending the Cyprians' Ball? Courtney didn't think it was likely anyone would send their daughters to her, but there was no reason to discuss that now. As long as she was staying, there was no reason for him to linger at Nanny's tonight, either. No honorable reason, that is. "Excellent. I'll be going, then. Good night, Miss Kathlyn Partland, and thank you."

Then he took her in his arms and kissed her good-bye. He hadn't meant to do it, knew he shouldn't do it, and did it anyway. She was too blasted beautiful not to.

"But . . . but there's no one here to be impressed," Kathlyn said when she got her breath back.

Oh no? His lordship was barely breathing himself. "I'm sorry, it just seemed like the thing to do," he said, which was, he knew, an inordinately lame excuse for the inexcusable.

Because of the late hour, the champagne, the excitement of the evening, whatever, Kathlyn felt she had to say what was in her heart. "No, my lord, you needn't apologize. I think you've behaved admirably, in light of your great sacrifice."

Blast and botheration, Courtney thought, how did the female figure it out? Was his kiss so inexpert, then? Well, she was no one to judge, obviously not knowing where to put her hands or her tongue, for that matter.

"I'm sure the country owes you a great debt," she was going on.

"The country?"

"Why, yes, for if every other young man in your position were as noble and as brave, the world would be a far different place."

Less populated, at least. "Then you don't think I'm dicked in the nob?"

"Not at all. Other men in your situation would have retreated from society, grown bitter—"

"And blind."

"Blind? Your eyesight was affected, too? You poor, poor man." This time Kathlyn walked into his embrace, and this time Courtney made sure she figured out the proper responses, even if her conversation was as queer as Dick's hatband.

"Are we going in?" Ripken wanted to know.

"What, interrupt a toff in his tupping? The swell's a viscount, you noddy; he'd be waiting on the governor's doorstep tomorrow morning, demanding our heads. You'd be searching for stolen cows out to Cornwall, and it wouldn't matter that you are 'is nibs's nevvy."

The two were in the hired hackney, a few doors from where Miss Partland and her paramour had left their carriage. They also happened to be a few blocks from Dimm's own house, so he was in an expansive mood, having ridden home at the government's expense.

"I say we go roust them out and search for the jewels."

"She weren't wearing them, that was for sure. And any thief as clever as Miss Partland would be too downy to stash the goods in her own mattress. 'Sides, we ain't got a warrant, or did you forget about the law already?"

"So we're going to let her get away?"

"Our kitty ain't going nowhere, not with the bed of catnip she's found for herself. She'll be here in the morning, after you get us a writ to search the premises. You go along now, take the hackney out of here. I'll bide over to the corner a spell just to make sure, then walk on home. Won't get her spooked or nothing, iffen she notices, which I doubt, Miss Partland being otherwise occupied."

Ripken watched the silhouetted couple kiss in the sheer-curtained window. He grinned. "Turning into a Peeping Tom in your dotage, eh, old man?"

"Refreshing my memory, is all. Now get on with you

afore someone in the neighborhood looks out to see why our cab is still here."

After Ripken left, Inspector Dimm crossed the street and lit his pipe. He stood in the shadows puffing, thinking, maybe even remembering nights when he had more to go home to than his cat. So he saw that second, longer, embrace, when a pigeon feather couldn't have slipped between the two lovers. And then he saw his lordship leave, limping down the street.

"Gorblimey, the bloke's attics are to let." Dimm didn't think any red-blooded—or blue-blooded—gent would let a sore leg keep him from that beauty's bed. He scratched his head.

There'd been odd stories about this lordling circulating around Bow Street once Chase was identified as the chit's protector, but no one put much stock in the prattle. The viscount was a decorated hero, with no other hint of scandal except a broken engagement. 'Sides, Dimm had seen that kiss. Lord Chase's limp hadn't shown there, nor any limp wrist. No, the Runner'd go bail his lordship's leg was the only thing not working properly. And maybe his brain box.

He was a Bedlamite, he had to be, to walk away like that. Blast it, though, Courtney thought, he wouldn't patronize the boudoirs and bordellos; he sure as hell wasn't going to start debauching innocents. He hadn't even made love to his own fiancée, for which he daily gave thanks since he'd have found himself honor-bound to marry the jade willy-nilly. Miss Partland couldn't drag him to the altar, didn't have a papa with a pistol, but she was a decent girl who deserved better.

She was also upstairs in her bed, crying her eyes out over what could never be. Being thrust out into the world hadn't disconcerted her, sharing a coach seat with a dead man hadn't discomposed her, but yearning for the unattainable just might destroy her.

Courtney couldn't sleep either. He got out of bed and

read a journal. Then he poured himself a drink. Then he wrote some notes for his estate manager. Then he decided that celibacy was for saints. If God had wanted Courtney Choate to be chaste, He wouldn't have put creatures like Kathlyn Partland in his path. So Courtney set out, at two in the morning, to end a lifetime's loyalty to the woman who would someday become his wife, whoever she might be.

The hired coach was halfway to an elegant establishment that catered to the most discriminating clientele when Lord Chase rapped on the roof with his cane and directed the jarvey to deliver him to White's. One more day. He'd try to get through one more night. To do it, he didn't want to see a woman, hear a woman, or smell a woman. Lily of the valley, he thought Kathlyn used. Damn.

White's wasn't very crowded, not on the night of the Paphians' party. Every member so inclined was somewhere enjoying the tidbit he'd selected from the bachelor fare on display in the Argyle Rooms. Half might still be in the Argyle Rooms, for all Courtney knew, passed out under the punch tables or coupling in dark corners. Happily, he'd taken Kitty out of there on the stroke of midnight, before the serious business of pleasure began.

Courtney was surprised to see his friends Woodbury and Lowe playing dice at White's, but not as surprised as they were to see him.

"Devil a bit, old man, how could you part from that angel so soon?" Algie wanted to know, and Woody fervently declared, "Miss Kitty couldn't need her beauty rest. She's already got every other female beat to flinders. Algie's been buying the rounds on his winnings."

"You mean you put money on Miss—on Kitty? Blast, she's a woman, not a racehorse! Just because she showed up at the Argyle Rooms doesn't mean she's a commodity."

"No reason to get in a snit, old man, no disrespect intended. I was betting on you, your taste, anyway, not the lady. You didn't let me down, Court, knew you wouldn't. Have a drink on me."

Another man at the table snickered. "Perhaps the viscount let the doxy down. He couldn't have tired her out already."

Lord Chase took his quizzing glass from his pocket and polished it carefully before holding it to his eye to inspect the insect who'd spoken. "Jepperson, is it? I suggest you crawl back under your rock. I can ignore your slurs on my manhood because I don't have to prove anything to the likes of you. I didn't notice you leading any charges at Coruña or Oporto."

An officer in scarlet uniform had also been casting the ivories. He stood and shouted, "Here, here! Honor of the regiment."

Courtney shoved the lieutenant back in his seat before he fell down. "As I said, Jepperson, your opinion of me matters less than nothing. I shall not, however, tolerate your aspersions on Miss Parke. The lady"—he emphasized *lady*—"is a very good friend of mine."

Woody jumped up. "And mine."

"And mine," Algie chimed in. "Kitty's a right 'un, with more sense than my own sisters."

Lieutenant Hydock stood up again. "Any friend of Captain Choate's is a friend of mine," he said, one hand on his dress sword, the other on a bottle of port. "Best damned officer in the cavalry."

Not yet recognizing his imminent demise, Jepperson took another mouthful of brandy and sneered. "What kind of lady goes to the Cyprians' Ball?"

A friend of Jepperson's added, "What kind of man turns his back on a prime article who does?"

They were all thrown out of the venerable club for brawling, which at least released some of Courtney's pent-up energies and emotions. The three friends, along with the lieutenant, stood on the walkway trying to decide which less reputable gaming establishment to patronize next. None of them was ready for home and bed, not with victory—and brandy—coursing through their blood. While Woody and Hydock argued the merits of the Coco Tree or McAlpin's, Courtney asked Algie what he'd been doing at White's. "I thought you were leaving the ball with that blonde."

Algie shrugged. "She didn't look so pretty in better light. And she didn't seem so attractive after seeing your, ah, lady friend, either."

So Woody pulled out a flask and they all drank a toast to Kitty, who was safe in her virginal bed, crying her eyes out.

Chapter Fourteen

At least there was ice. The damned winter weather was good for something. As they walked, the four men gathered up handfuls of slush and broke off icicles from the eaves and fence grilles where the melting snow had refrozen. They wrapped the stuff in lace-edged, mono-grammed handkerchiefs, and applied it to Woody's swelling eye, Algie's split lip, Courtney's bloody knuckles, and the lieutenant's nose, which they did not think was broken. The other patrons of Hamlet's gave the quartet a wide berth except for a red-haired serving girl with half-unlaced bodice who came to ask their pleasure. She addressed all of them, but looked only at Courtney.

"He's already had his fill for the night," the lieutenant slurred. "Broke m'beak provin' it. My turn." So the wench took Hydock upstairs, to tend to his poor nose and his purse.

The viscount was aggravated. He'd wanted male com-panionship, not reminders of male concupiscence. He hadn't wanted to come to any place so inauspiciously named as Hamlet's anyway, having had quite enough of that to-be-or-not-to-be folderol.

"It ain't that kind of Hamlet," Woody urged. "Used to

be called the Pigsty, but no one wanted to eat in such a place. You'll see."

What the viscount saw was a narrow corridor with a long wooden bar to one side, low-ceilinged and smoke-filled. What he heard were squeals and grunts from the room beyond. Wallowing indeed. Still, he followed his friends through the curtained door.

It really was a pigsty. There were tables and chairs where customers ate and drank, but there was also a pen full of piglets to one side, and a large barricaded dirt oval in the middle.

They took a table and gave their orders to a big, cauliflower-eared man in a dirty apron, who glared suspiciously at their bruises.

"No trouble," he warned, "no credit, and no one messes with the pigs. We run an honest track here."

"Never tell me they race the creatures," Courtney said when the fellow left after seeing their blunt. "Pigs?"

Algie was enthusiastic. "Why not? They give them names, dress them in coats with numbers on them, take bets, and send them 'round. There's a bucket of mash at the other end, so the little porkers are eager to run. The winners get better odds the next heat, and the losers—" He picked up a pork chop from his plate and shrugged. "Not much different from horse racing."

"Of course it is! The sport of kings has decades of breeding going into each horse, track records, practice times. Why, picking a winner is a regular science."

"Not the way we manage to lose. If it weren't for the pater being so generous, my pockets would be permanently to let. Woody's got his aunt Aurelia to keep him out of River Tick."

Courtney shook his head. "It's no wonder you're always dipped, the way you two nodcocks will bet on anything. But this, this is picking a pig in a poke. Literally."

Woody was staring at the chalkboard, his mouth hanging open. "They've got names, Court." He fished in his pockets, pulling out his watch, a snuffbox, a bit of broken harness, coins, and calling cards. "I know I wrote it down, damn it. What did she say?"

"Are you sure you don't need a physician, Woody? Maybe that blow to your head . . . ? Only a blackguard like Jepperson would have picked up the chair that way."

"Your lady friend, you dolt! Madame Katerina picked the winners for me."

"You really are delirious, you know. Kitty can't tell the future any more than these pigs can fly."

But Woody'd found his note. "The fastest, the luckiest, gold and scarlet." He scrutinized the entry board even harder. The piglets for the first race were Sir Roger, Skytrotter, Pinky, and Master Speed. Master Speed won, of course, as did Lucky Bedeviled in the next race. Brass Knuckles won his heat, in his gold silks, and Sower Cherry hers, in red. Woody had a pile of coins and bills in front of him, and a fervid gleam in his one open eye.

"Epsom, Court. You've got to bring Kitty to Epsom. She'll make our fortunes, I know it."

"Don't be a clunch. It was sheer coincidence. I swear to you, Kitty can't pick winners."

"Picked you, didn't she?"

Which left Courtney with nothing to say but that ladies didn't go to Epsom.

"No offense, old man," Algie put in, ready to duck under the table if Courtney came up swinging, "but ladies like m'sisters don't go to the track. Ladies like Miss Kitty do. 'Struth."

Blast! Courtney couldn't claim that Kitty was as pure as the driven snow, not after dragging her through the mud of London's demimonde, and not after using her to establish his reputation as a premier rake.

"If you want, I'll invite that blonde along so Miss Kitty won't feel so alone."

Miss Partland sharing a carriage seat with a two-bit Haymarket whore? Courtney choked on his sliced ham. "Sorry, we have other plans."

"Well, change 'em." Algie slapped him on the back, a

trifle harder than necessary. "It ain't as if you're taking her to meet your mother or anything. We need her, Court. Quarter day's a long time off."

"No, I'm sorry to disoblige, especially after you took on half of White's for me, but it's just not possible. I, uh, have commitments with my man of business. Investments, don't you know. Interviewing a new steward for the property in Derby, and, yes, an appointment at the War Office. Can't miss that, or they'll take back my medals. Mean to put in a good word for Hydock while I'm there, too." He wiped his brow.

Algie and Woody were convinced—that the viscount couldn't go to Epsom with them. "We'll take Miss Kitty ourselves, then. Only be gone a few days and you'll hardly notice, you're so busy. Wouldn't want her to sit around Town by herself, would you?"

"I swear to take as good care as if she were one of m'sisters, so you don't have to worry she'll take up with some other chap."

The viscount was so outraged, he was sputtering: "You . . . you henwits are suggesting taking Miss . . . my mistress away with you?"

"Devil a bit, old man, no need to get in a pucker. We only want to borrow the chit for a few days. Bring her right back, all safe and sound, 'pon rep."

"Borrow? By heaven, she's not a jar of snuff to be passed around and sampled. She's a person, a woman with a mind of her own who makes her own choices and picks her own friends. And I say she's not going. In fact, I'd better stop in on her now, see if she's over that, ah, headache she had earlier."

"Jar of snuff can't pick winners," Woody mumbled as Lord Chase paid his shot and left.

Algie just shook his head. "You know a fellow has it bad for a chit when he starts believing his doxy is a duchess. Nice gal and all, happy he's found a female who suits, but she ain't any Adelina Marlowe."

"I'll drink to that."

So they did, but after a few more rounds and a few more pig races, which they lost, they were still blue-deviled that Courtney was too selfish to let them take Miss Kitty to Epsom.

So they decided to kidnap her.

"I tell you, Ursula, the Runner's flunky didn't find nothin' up north. Quigley an' me heard him tell the old gaffer in the park. 'Sides, I seen him diggin' around, callin' again on the old besom what put out the reward, the one what misplaced her jewels, kind of."

"Well, the girl ain't got the diamonds."

Sean wasn't convinced. He was cold, tired, hungry, and mad that Ursula wouldn't let him and Quigley stay at her place, where they could keep an eye more on the wily widow and less on the wildlife. "How can you be sure, Ursie, just 'cause she wasn't wearin' 'em last night?"

" 'Cause I asked, you looby. Described them to her, and she never batted an eye. 'Sides, do you think any female'd be needing a protector if she had Harry's horde? She could open her own house if she was so inclined. But that ain't Kitty's style, no more'n it's her name from on the waybill. Missy was too high in the instep to dance with strangers; she ain't going to be taking them home. It's a gold ring a female like that wants. Her viscount might be a pretty fellow, but he ain't going to marry her, no matter how he doesn't take his blue eyes off her."

"Not even if she's got a fortune in jewels?" Quigley didn't think any man could be that stupid.

Ursula knew better. "Nob like that don't marry his mistress. He can be a regular hell-raker, but his wife's got to be snow white. No, if she had the rocks, Kitty'd set herself up somewheres as a respectable widow and find herself a husband. She sure as hell wouldn't keep working on her back, I can vouch for that."

Sean didn't want to give up. He didn't want to go back

picking pockets, either. "Maybe she ain't had a chance to go get the sparklers yet."

"Trust me, if the Gypsy knew where the gems were, she'd grow wings."

"So what are we goin' to do?" Quigley scratched his head in thought. Then he scratched his arm, his back, and his leg. "We ain't got the jewels, ain't got no money, and you ain't got the brains to plan another burglary. Why'd you have to go and kill old Harry, Sean?" He cuffed the shorter man on the ear, killing a flea or two.

" 'Cause he was cuttin' out on us, without cuttin' up the loot. We wouldn't of been no better off."

But Ursula would have been, with Harry or with the reward money. She was finding the high life harder now that her breasts were lower and her belly was softer. Only wait till that hoity-toity Gypsy saw a few more birthdays, Ursula thought, a few more lines, a few more pounds. There wouldn't be any blond Adonis hovering over her then, no broad-shouldered nabob like the one who wouldn't even look at Ursula at the ball.

"It's all that female's fault, and Harry's for dying in her arms. There's got to be a way to make some money off her."

"But how'll we find her, Ursula? You were too busy with that tall, skinny cove to notice where she went."

"That tall, skinny cove is a lordship, you bacon-brain, and he's that viscount's friend. He's heading for Epsom tomorrow, and I just might invite myself along. He'll tell me everything we need to know. You two worthless wantwits can keep an eye on the Runners in the meantime, and the park, in case Chase takes his fancy piece out for an airing."

"Then what?"

"Then either we shake the jewels out of her or we find out how hard that pretty nobleman will come down to get her back. He looked top over tails to me. That ought to be worth a penny or two."

"Nob ain't goin' to ransom no trull. He can get any

116

woman he wants for a song. Why should he empty his pockets for this one? You said yourself he was too proud."

"And I said he was moonstruck, too. Fellow in love just might put the dibs in tune. If not, we sell her to one of the flash houses, and I'll get to comfort the viscount when his Gypsy don't come home."

So they decided to kidnap her.

In the north of England, Manchester to be exact, another woman was making plans for Kathlyn's future. Madorra, Lady Bellamy, had discounted the Runner's reports that her niece was in London. The dunderhead couldn't find her jewels; what was he doing finding something she hadn't lost? Then she received an express from one of her bosom bows, saying that a female the spit and image of her estranged sister Gwyneth was seen in Town, at the Opera, the Royal Academy, and the museum, with a prominent bachelor, sans chaperone.

Lady Bellamy had to resort to her smelling salts—and she hadn't even heard about the Cyprians' Ball. That would have called for burnt feathers. A whole down pillow full.

It had to be Gwyneth's daughter her friend had seen. Who else would be so headstrong and hey-go-mad, like her mother, who had run off to marry a penniless tutor instead of the fine match their father had arranged, bringing disgrace to them all. Why, Lord Bellamy had almost cried off from allying his name—and fortune—to such a scandal. Now Gwyneth's daughter was going to shame them all worse, for she wasn't marrying beneath her, she wasn't marrying at all! And here Lady Bellamy had two daughters to bring out this season who would be tarred by the same brush. Vinaigrette wasn't enough; Madorra needed her lordship's cognac.

What to do, what to do. She obviously had to get the girl out of London before the Season began. Ladies might turn their backs and pretend that such females did not exist, but one was always tripping over them in the park, at the theater or the modistes'. And if rumor was correct that this Kathlyn was half as beautiful as her mother, she'd be noticed. And recognized.

She could have taken the girl in with them after Partland died, made her an unpaid companion of sorts, but what did Madorra want with a chit prettier than her own lambs? Especially with Bellamy as randy as a goat. Lady Bellamy would have had all the expense and bother of finding her niece some clerk or tenant farmer to wed. Worse, she'd have had her at home, underfoot, for an entire year of mourning for that ne'er-do-well who hadn't bothered to arrange his daughter's future before sticking his spoon in the wall. The gel was one and twenty, by heaven. If he'd ever taken his beaky nose out of a book, Partland could have found someone to take the girl off his hands even without a dowry, if she was the beauty the rumor mill reported.

Well, Gwyneth's brat had to be got out of the way before she landed them all in the scandalbroth. Since he wasn't having to pay out the reward for her stolen diamonds, Bellamy might be willing to buy the chit passage to the Americas. Yes, that's what she'd do, even if she had to kidnap the girl.

When Kathlyn finally went to sleep, her dreams were troubled. A whole pack of rats was chasing after her. No, they were vultures, maybe spiders, things with claws and fangs and little beady eyes that glowed in the dark. They were calling her name and reaching out for her, closer, closer. If she could get to Lord Chase, she'd be safe, she knew, but he kept walking away, despite her cries. Then he heard her and turned. There was a big hole where his heart should have been.

Kathlyn woke up in a sweat, as though she'd been running. The day was as gray as her thoughts, but it didn't look like rain or snow, so she went early to take Nanny's grandchildren for a walk before their lessons. She needed to let their sweetness wash away the nightmare, and their innocence wash away the heartbreak, before she was lost indeed. It didn't take any Gypsy soothsayer to interpret that dream or predict her future. No, she couldn't stay on in London. But where was she going to go?

Chapter Fifteen

"*I*ce? You had a carriage accident on the ice and Lord Chase reinjured his leg? Oh dear."

Kathlyn had been walking back from Mrs. Dawson's daughter's house when a closed carriage pulled alongside her. She was hailed by the two men on the driver's seat, who turned out to be Lord Algernon Lowe and Sir Vernon Woodbury, looking battered themselves.

Algie and Woody had found their quarry by accident, Courtney's footman having refused to divulge her address even for a bribe, and his driver not buying their story about returning a lost fan to his lordship's companion of the night before. The viscount's friends knew he had a place in Kensington, though—everyone knew that—and Kensington wasn't all that big, they decided. So they drove up and down the streets, hoping to spot someone to ask the whereabouts of a raven-haired dazzler with black-rimmed blue eyes. Any lad who'd seen her was bound to take note of her direction.

They did better, the would-be abductors, finding Kitty walking by herself. Nanny had done her marketing this morning, Meg's, too, and the maid Lizzie was home with a sore throat. By chance, Kathlyn was alone.

"See? Didn't I tell you, Algie? If she's not a fortune-teller, at least she's good luck." And they proceeded to convince her to go with them to Courtney's aid.

"But surely Mrs. Dawson would be a better choice." Kathlyn pointed back toward Meg's house.

"What, he's got another female on the line?" Algie asked his cohort too low for Kathlyn's hearing. "Then old Court had no call to be so possessive of this one."

"Right, won't miss her at all."

Algie climbed down to assist Kathlyn into the carriage while moon-faced Woody held the ribbons. "But it's you he's calling for, ma'am. The surgeon said to set his mind at rest, so here we are."

"He'll be all right?"

"If we keep him quiet, Miss Parke, otherwise all that thrashing about . . ." Algie shrugged his thin shoulders. "Who knows?"

As Kathlyn stepped up, he asked which house was hers. "For you might want to pack a few personal items, don't you know, in case you're at Cho—: House a few days."

Kathlyn stepped back, aghast. "Days? I cannot stay at his house overnight!"

Misinterpreting, Algie told her, "Of course you can. His mama ain't in residence."

"But my rep—" No, she had none, in his friends' eyes. "Surely his lordship has a valet, a butler, or factotum at least, some servant who could sit up with him."

"Needs a woman's touch, he does. Bound to get delirious come midnight, don't you know. Nothing more calming than a woman's voice."

Kathlyn made one last try. "His housekeeper?"

"But it's you he keeps crying out for. Piteous, it is, too, him in that much pain. Says he won't take the laudanum until you get there. Stubborn chap, old Courtney."

"Mutton-headed mule, more like," she muttered, getting in and giving directions to Nanny's house.

Kathlyn tossed a shawl into her carpetbag, her comb and brush, night robe, and a change of undergarments.

The coins from her Gypsy palm-reading went into her reticule, her book into a cloak pocket when Kathlyn remembered the long hours at her father's bedside trying to stay awake in case he needed a cool drink or his medication. She didn't stay to pack anything else or write a note; Algie said it would be faster to send a messenger back from Choate House, and time was of the essence.

She did hear noises from the rear of the house, though. Perhaps Nanny was returned, or Lizzie felt better, she thought, racing to the kitchen with her hair flying and her satchel bouncing at her side and Algie hurrying to keep her from getting away.

The only ones in the kitchen, however, were Wolfie the dog and Little George, who was, of course, deaf and dumb. So Kathlyn pointed at herself and Algie, who was sidling back down the hall at sight of Little George's bulk and the old dog's gums. Then she started limping, to indicate that she was going to the viscount's. George nodded and went back to splitting kindling. Wolfie went back to sleep.

Kathlyn didn't notice the trunks strapped to the back of the carriage, nor the hamper of food placed inside. She didn't even think it odd that Algie rejoined Sir Vernon on the box rather than keeping her company in the coach. They must be too upset for their friend to fret over the niceties, too. Oh, that poor man, how he must be suffering. Well, Kathlyn certainly couldn't leave London now.

An hour later she realized she had, indeed, left London. Choate House in Mayfair couldn't be nearly so far, nor were they traveling at a rate of speed suitable for the city. She started banging on the roof with her book of sonnets, the only thing she could find.

"Don't worry, Miss Kitty," one of the nodcocks shouted back. "It's merely an adventure."

Oh, dear. Those two rattles had stolen her away as a prank to tease Lord Chase. No, it must have been a wager, knowing Algie and Woody. They'd never see reason, she knew, at least not until they stopped to change horses and she could give them a piece of her mind. With nothing else to do, Kathlyn curled up on the velvet seats and tried to catch up on last night's lost sleep, now that she didn't have to worry about his lordship.

"I declare, I cannot imagine what his lordship is going to say, officers with warrants in his house." Nanny was beside herself. She didn't even offer the Runners tea, to Inspector Dimm's regret, especially when he smelled gingerbread cooking in this cozy little place that was neat as a pin. His hadn't been so tidy since his sister-in-law who kept house for him up and remarried. Hadn't had gingerbread since the last young'un moved out either.

At least this Mrs. Dawson wasn't keeping him and Ripken standing out on the stoop. Dimm had been waiting for Ripken at the corner, where it was so cold, his spectacles kept getting too foggy for him to see, and his joints were freezing him into a demmed statue. If he solved this case and earned the reward, b'gad, he was going to emigrate to Jamaica. Of course, if he didn't solve this case, he just might be exiled to Antarctica. His nibs hadn't been happy with their serving a warrant at a viscount's house. He was going to be less happy. The viscount was not there; neither was the girl.

"Aha!" was all Ripken had to say.

Mrs. Dawson turned on him, brandishing her broom. "She's at my daughter's house, teaching my grandchildren their letters. What's untoward about that?"

Dimm inched nearer the fire, keeping a wary eye on Mrs. Dawson, who looked like she wanted to sweep them away like specks of dirt that dared mess up her parlor. "Nothing untoward, ma'am, we just need to speak to the young woman."

"Then why do you and this jackanapes have a warrant to search her room?"

"Well, ma'am, it's like this. . . ." Dimm proceeded to

tell her about the dead thief, the missing jewels, and the reward, watching for her reaction.

She was outraged. "Miss Kathlyn has nothing to do with anything like that. She's a dear, decent girl, and I'll challenge anyone who says otherwise, so there."

"Decent?" Ripken said with a sneer to his lip. "A female of easy virtue might get up to any number of indecent, even criminal acts."

Nanny advanced on him, the broom handle pointing like a spear at his midsection. "I'll have you know Miss Kathlyn is a good girl, and I won't hear any talk of easy virtue in my house, young man. She might have her own reasons for tricking herself out like a Gypsy, but it couldn't be helped, with no one to look after the chick but my lad."

"Your lad?" Dimm shoved Ripken into a corner, out of Mrs. Dawson's range.

"Master Courtney, Viscount Chase to you, sirrah, him what I gave my own milk when he was an infant. I've known and loved him ever since, and I won't hear a word against him either. Gave me this house to live in, he did, and makes sure I don't have a worry in the world."

Ripken couldn't keep his mouth shut. "How many other pieces of muslin does he bring here?"

Nanny poked him in the chest until he was backed against the mantel, the back of his trousers perilously close to the grate. "Your mama would be ashamed, young man. Go on, go look, and then get out of my house."

Miss Partland's room was a bit messy, especially compared to the rest of the house, but Mrs. Dawson explained that her maid Lizzie was home, sick. While Ripken searched the clothespress, Dimm noticed that there were no combs or brushes on the dresser, but Nanny explained that away, too: Kathlyn had such long hair, she just braided it in the morning for the children, intending to do it up proper over at Meg's, in case his lordship was taking her out later. What Nanny couldn't rationalize to herself, and wouldn't think of discussing with the Runners, was the fact that Kathlyn's warm robe was missing, too, and her valise.

Ripken kept muttering about all the expensive fripperies in the drawers, and Nanny kept glaring at him for what he was thinking. "You can get your mind out of the gutter, you young twit. Nothing like that goes on under my roof, by all that's holy. Because missy's got no family to speak of and has to earn her keep doesn't mean she's sold her virtue. And Master Courtney wouldn't bring his fancy piece here. I hope I taught the boy better than that. She's doing him a favor, is all, going about with him, and it's little minds what think anything else. Little minds and little men."

They didn't find any jewels.

There was nothing for it but to go out in the cold. "We'll go talk with Miss Partland at your daughter's then, ma'am, if you give us her direction."

"You won't find her. Miss Kathlyn takes the children to the park so my Meg can rest. She's feeling poorly and I won't have her disturbed. You don't have a warrant to go *there*, do you?"

Dimm sighed. This line of work was a lot harder when folks hated them. Nipperkin had a lot to learn. "Do you mind if we wait here for her?"

"Yes, I do." Nanny needed to send for his lordship on the instant. "I have a great many chores and then my daughter's household to see to. You've had your search, and your unlicked cub's got his pleasure touching a lady's dainties. Nothing in that bit of paper you showed me gives you the right to litter up my sitting room."

"We're only trying to do our job, ma'am, protecting the populace. That includes you and Miss Partland. She could be in danger, you know."

"Go on with you. Who'd ever want to hurt a sweet child like that?"

"The Diamond Mine gang, ma'am, them as stole the jewels, or what's left of them. They've been seen around." He consulted his Occurrence book. "A short, ugly-tempered fellow, a taller one what's missing part of his ear, and a yellow-haired female. Don't suppose you've seen any of them lurking around the neighborhood?"

"Heavens, no!"

"Well, they want the missing stones, too, so's they can cut them up and sell them. Killed their own ringleader over them, shot a guard. Now, if we know Miss Partland's here, so do they."

Nanny sank down on the sofa, her hand over her heart. "That poor dearie. What should we do?" Forgotten was her intention of sending for the viscount or throwing these public servants out. "You have to keep her safe."

"That chore'd be a mite easier if you let us wait here and talk to the closest thing to a witness we have, see if she remembers anything else about Harry Miner . . . or her aunt's jewels."

"Her aunt?"

"Lady Bellamy—it was her husband what brought the Bellamy Diamonds back from India—was sister to Kathlyn Partland's mum. Their da was Lord Fowler."

"I knew our Kitty was Quality! Why, that changes everything."

"Doesn't help find the jewels or catch the criminals, ma'am," Dimm said while Ripken looked behind the sofa cushions. All he found was Wolfie's latest bone, which didn't sit too well with Wolfie. Mrs. Dawson patted the old dog on the head, then she patted Dimm on the shoulder. "You'll work it out, dearie, I know you will." Next she went off to the kitchen to fix them tea while they waited. Dimm could swear he heard her singing, and right after him telling her a band of cutthroats could be landing on her doorstep. He shook his head. He wasn't going to understand women—ever, not even on the day he died.

He'd bet his good-luck piece that Mrs. Dawson wasn't any procuress, though, and this wasn't any house of iniquity. What kind of bordello kept a smelly old dog to stain the carpet? It was a kind heart she had, the viscount's nanny, noticing the pipe in his pocket and inviting him to light it in the house. Even his darling Cora, God keep her, made him smoke in the garden. Maybe that's why his joints ached so now. Mrs. Dawson asked about his family, too, and they laughed in agreement that surely grandchildren were a gift from heaven, and it was heaven when they went home to their mamas.

Dimm couldn't help comparing this rounded, gray-haired woman in her neat apron to that veiled widow in the park who'd been dropping her handkerchief for him to pick up. Mrs. Dawson was too intelligent to ask an old gaffer like him to bend down so far. The widow was younger by decades, more shapely, more seductive. Dimm bet she couldn't find her way around a kitchen.

Nanny brought out a tray heaped with gingerbread and apple butter to go on top, poppy-seed cake, and maca-roons. Any woman who cooked this good had to be telling the truth.

Chapter Sixteen

'*T*was an ill wind that blew no one any good, but this one did Kathlyn a favor. It blew snow, sleet, and rain hard enough to cancel that day's racing. Algie and Woody wouldn't take her home, but they did hire her the finest bedroom at the Pegasus Inn and a maid to wait on her. The viscount would have naught to complain of in their treatment of his property, they assured each other. Of course, the two did expect Miss Kitty to join them in their private parlor for dinner and to study the racing forms for the next day's races.

She'd be wasting her breath to tell the viscount's bacon-brained friends that it was not proper for her to sit alone with two unattached males. They thought she'd done a lot more than sit alone with Lord Chase. For his sake, and for her given word, Kathlyn could not disabuse them of the notion that she was a fallen woman. She did not have to conduct herself like one, however.

"I am sorry, gentlemen, but I cannot join you for dinner. I have no appropriate attire." She fingered the shabby fabric of her old gray kerseymere, the only one of her old gowns that she'd saved, to play in with the children.

"Thought of that, Miss Kitty," Algie said proudly.

"Brought along some of m'sisters' frocks. The brats have so many, they won't miss a few."

"Oh, but I couldn't—"

"Then we won't change for dinner either, eh, Woody? Be a pleasure, not getting rigged out like a Tulip for once. Of course, we'll all have to sup upstairs in your room then, so we can plan our strategy for the races."

Put like that, Kathlyn allowed as how she'd change and meet them downstairs in an hour.

The serving girl who brought her hot water and stayed to do up her buttons refused to remain with Kathlyn in the private parlor, not even for the coins Kathlyn offered.

"Gents in the taproom'll pay a lot more'n that, iffen you get my drift." Her wink said she believed Kathlyn understood very well. "Onct you decide which of your bucks to have, you can send t'other one to me. But if your boyo gets out of hand, you call for Sal. He won't put up with rough stuff, iffen it disturbs the other customers. A'course, you look like you can handle them two. Have 'em eatin' out of the palm of your hand in that rig." She made a face at her own black skirt and dingy apron, then waited impatiently for Kathlyn to follow her to the private parlor.

Giving one last look in the small, blackened mirror, Kathlyn shrugged and followed. Everyone thought she was a whore. Now she looked the part.

Algie's sisters were debutantes, sixteen and seventeen years of age, so their gowns were virginal white, with ribbons and rosebuds, ruffles, and ruched hems. Naturally Algie hadn't thought to bring the lace petticoats that went under a scalloped hem, so Kathlyn's ankles showed. That wasn't all that showed. Those teenaged sisters were girls, not yet reaching their mature proportions. Kathlyn was a woman. Most definitely a woman.

Algie turned red, Woody couldn't speak at all, and the manservant bringing dinner walked into the door on his way out. Kathlyn hoped Lord Chase would be proud of his handiwork.

"Is that hot rum punch I see, gentlemen? Do you know, I don't believe I've ever tasted any." Since she couldn't change the situation—or anyone's mind—Kathlyn decided she may as well enjoy herself for the one night. Tomorrow Miss Kathlyn Partland would find her way back to London even if she had to walk, in her own gray kerseymere, thank you, but for tonight she was Kitty Parke, mistress to the most attractive, generous man in London. She hadn't a worry in the world, not her future, not her nonexistent reputation, and not the amorous advances of these two gambling fools. Their own sort of gentlemanly honor protected her, belonging as she did to their good friend Courtney. So all she had to do was eat, drink, pray the roads didn't get washed away, and keep these two paperskulls from losing their patrimonies at the track on the morrow.

An hour passed while they explained the nuances of all the information given on a tout sheet, then she was supposed to pick the winners. Kathlyn hadn't a clue.

"Here, have another cup of punch. It'll help you relax. Now, what do you see?"

"I see the walls whirling around."

"Blister it, Woody, you've given her too much to drink."

But Woody was consulting the racing forms. There was a Whirligig in the first, but the gelding was racing against Stonewall. "Go on, Kitty. Close your eyes, maybe something else will come to you."

What came to her was the image of a tall, fair-haired man with a limp, and a dimple when he smiled. She'd give anything to have him smile at her right now, to have his eyes light up at the sight of her in this outlandishly revealing garment. "Chase," she blurted, then clapped her hands over her mouth. Oh dear, now she was thinking like a fallen woman, too.

"Tagg in the second, good job, Kitty!"

But nothing else came after that, no intuition and no images of dashing Gypsy gentlemen, because Kathlyn refused to entertain such forward thoughts. Instead she was close to drifting off to sleep.

Algie wandered out to the taproom, in search of something to inspire her psychic powers, he said. He came back with Mina, the blond woman whose palm Madame Katerina had read at the Argyle Rooms. Mina seemed to be inspiring Algie, all right, as they returned to the private parlor arm in arm.

Harry Miner's widow stopped dead in her tracks when she saw Kathlyn, for whom Sean and Quigley were right now searching—in London. "You do get around, don't you, ducks?"

Kathlyn nodded. "And you, ma'am. Have you come upon your diamonds yet?"

"Not hide nor hair, and you?"

"Sparkle My Lady in the third, or Bijou in the fourth?"

Ursula turned to stare at Woody, wondering what the high-flying chit, whatever she called herself today, was doing with this baby-faced buffoon. What happened to the pretty toff with the limp and the longing looks? No female was dicked in the nob enough to pick this gaby over the viscount. He'd never get a girl's blood pumping, and he'd never go bail for a ransom demand either, more's the pity.

While Ursula was trying to hint the tall, skinny gent into a corner and into revealing what this unlikely trio was doing together, Kathlyn slipped away upstairs to her bedroom. She locked the door, then moved a chair under it, and made sure the window was too high off the ground to offer any danger. She decided to sleep in the white gown; she would be ready for any eventuality, and she wouldn't have to ring for that brazen maid to come undo her buttons. She put her own robe over it and climbed into bed with her book of sonnets. She'd been in the habit of reading almost daily, and missed it, but her eyes were growing heavy after the first page. How odd, she thought briefly, Nanny's grandchildren must have taken a pencil to her book, or perhaps it was Lizzie, trying to learn her letters, who had underlined some words she didn't recognize. Kathlyn blew out the candle. She'd think about it in the morning, right after she figured out how to get back to London.

"She what?" Courtney's head ached, his mouth felt as if some small, scaly creature had shed its skin there, and his clothing was sopping wet after racing across town in a deluge in response to Nanny's urgent summons. The world was making no sense. Governesses, even ones hired to imitate intimate associates, did not run off with jewel thieves. Nor did they get abducted by marauding gangs, as Nanny was wailing about. Who were these men in her parlor then, and where the deuce was Kitty? Blast, that woman attracted trouble like a magnet.

"Everyone stop shouting!" he shouted. Having been heard across battlefields and over cannon fire, he got the attention of everyone in the little room. He hadn't forgotten how to be a very commanding officer. "That's better. Now, let me get this straight. You, sir, are a representative of Bow Street's new police force?"

"Aye, Cap'n, Jeremiah Dimm, at your service."

Well, he wasn't, thought the viscount. If the white-haired man were at Courtney's service, he'd have had this whole mare's nest resolved hours ago, without disturbing Nanny. The Runner was very much at his own leisure, it appeared, pipe in hand, feet propped on the footstool, a few scattered crumbs on a dish at his side, and Wolfie's head on his knee.

"You're his assistant?"

"Ned Ripken, my lord. 'Twas I who made the connection between all the crimes. The way I see it—"

Courtney scowled at the young man. "Do you even shave yet?"

"No, my lord."

"Then sit down and keep your opinions to yourself until I ask for them. Now, you two gentlemen came here to ask Miss Kathlyn Partland about some missing jewels connected to a man she befriended on the mail coach to London. Is that correct, Mr. Dimm?" He addressed the senior investigator, with his eyes narrowed at the younger, daring him to speak out of order.

"Aye, Cap'n, in a nutshell, except the man was murdered and the jewels belonged to Miss Partland's maternal aunt."

"Her aunt who was Lord Fowler's daughter," Nanny Dawson put in, not fearing his lordship's temper one whit.

"I don't care if she was a guinea fowl's daughter. She couldn't be much of a relative, letting Kitty, Miss Partland, that is, go into service. That's neither here nor there. What does matter is that Miss Partland was not here to answer the questions, and hasn't come home yet."

"Right." Ripken jumped up, then cleared his throat. "Ah, that is correct, my lord." He pulled out his daybook and carefully read, "We arrived here at this residence at eleven o'clock. Miss Partland was not present. At twelve-thirty Miss Partland had not returned. I went to Mrs. Dawson's daughter's home, at number fifteen, Marion Lane, where I ascertained that the subject had been earlier and had left at approximately ten-fifteen. At one-thirty a message was sent to your other residence, my lord, in case the subject was, ah, spending the day in your company." He bowed before resuming his seat. "My lord."

Courtney looked to Dimm, who only puffed on his pipe and hunched his shoulders. "He'll outgrow it."

"If he lives so long," the viscount muttered. He turned to Nanny. "You said some of her things were missing?"

"Her comb and brush." Nanny wrung her hands on her apron. "And a robe and a valise."

"Aha!" Ripken was out of his seat again, despite the viscount's glare. "That means she packed. I was right, this was no abduction at all. The jade rejoined her gang. You better check your silver, Mrs. Dawson."

"When one of her new dresses left upstairs is worth more than all my belongings?" Nanny moved the tray of gingerbread farther out of his reach. "Use your brain, you chowderhead, if the good Lord gave you one."

Courtney was nibbling on a macaroon. "But where would she go in such a hurry, without leaving a note? I can't figure it out. Couldn't be another position, for I was going to furnish references."

Ripken mumbled to himself, "Didn't know toffs required references for their doxies."

Three pairs of eyes turned on him, and one growl. Wolfie hadn't forgiven the young Runner for snatching his bone. Ripken thought he might visit the necessary out back.

When he left, the viscount turned to Inspector Dimm. "Miss Partland is a governess. She is going to be a schoolteacher."

"If you say so, Cap'n. His nibs at Bow Street vouched for you. Hero and all, man of honor, he said. Howbeit, seems you ain't seen this morning's paper." He unfolded a sheet for the viscount's viewing. There was a drawing of Kathlyn in her Gypsy outfit, twenty gentlemen at her feet holding out their hands. The caption read "Me next."

She wasn't going to be a schoolteacher for anyone who read the newspapers. Courtney cleared his throat. "Well, ah, there was an, um, a bet, you see." Lord Chase wasn't in the habit of explaining himself, but there was something about Inspector Dimm, looking like a kindly old elf, that made him want to justify his actions. "Miss Partland needed a place to stay while she got herself established. She agreed to help me, in exchange." Blast, that sounded lame, even to Courtney's ears. The chit had no choice, adrift in London without any other lifeline to grab. He should have sent her right to his mother, or brought her to Nanny, handed her his purse, and turned his back. He hadn't, by Jupiter; he'd taken advantage of her innocence instead.

"She's not a jewel thief or a criminal, Inspector. She's not even a courtesan."

"Of course she's not. Dearie's Lord Fowler's grand-daughter," Nanny insisted.

Dimm merely nodded, puffed on his pipe, and repeated, "If you say so, Cap'n, as should know."

"I do say so, and I'll prove it if it's the last thing I do, once I find her."

The only problem was that no one knew where to start looking. Then Little George came into the room to replenish the coals. Now, Little George could neither speak nor hear, but he could draw up a storm. He handed Nanny his slate-board, covered with colored chalk marks. They all gathered around to look. There was a cat carrying a suitcase, getting into a coach drawn by four horses.

"That must be Kitty, leaving. But what are these other marks?" Nanny fished her spectacles out of her apron pocket. "They're two stick men, I think, wearing top hats and high collars. Gentlemen, George must mean. One's much taller than the other. Now, who could that be . . . ?"

Courtney tripped over Wolfie in his haste to get to the door. "My God, today is Friday. Epsom. I'll kill them."

"Remember she's Lord Fowler's granddaughter," Nanny called after him.

"She could be King George's granddaughter. If that peagoose went with those dolts voluntarily, I'll strangle her."

Chapter Seventeen

*W*ith every drop of freezing rain that dripped off his hat brim down his neck, with every pellet of sleet that stung his cheeks, Courtney's resolve hardened. Someone was going to pay for this nightmarish ride. Woe the stable-boy who didn't move fast enough. Pity the innkeeper late with his reckoning. As for Woody and Algie, dismemberment was sounding attractive. And if Lord Chase lamed his horse in this headlong gallop in murk and mud, those two cods-heads would be lucky to get off so easily. It was bad enough that the viscount himself was likely to be permanently crippled from this ride through hell, but his horse?

Nanny'd urged him to take the curricle, at least, to protect his injured leg and so he could bring Miss Kathlyn back with him. Dimm opted for the closed carriage, so he and his assistant could come along to prevent mayhem. Too dangerous, too slow, too much interference. He was a cavalry officer, by George, and he'd do things his own way.

Kathlyn wasn't sleeping well. She kept being disturbed by the loud noises coming from the public room below, the heavy boot-steps and high-pitched laughter on the stairs down the hall. As for the sounds from the room next door—she put her pillow over her head and tried to go back to sleep. She was safe, she told herself. The window was locked, the door was bolted. No one would bother one lone female, even in a disreputable place like this. Or would they?

Then Kathlyn heard a louder commotion, screams, breaking glass, and running feet. She jumped out of bed, lit her candle, and grabbed up the fireplace poker. Sure enough, someone was trying her door! Whoever it was pounded on the thin wood and bellowed, "If you don't open this door, I'll knock it down."

The intruder sounded like an ogre from under a bridge, over the landlord's shouts, a woman's shrieking, someone else's moaning.

"If you do, I'll . . . I'll shoot," Kathlyn quavered back, vowing to purchase a pistol before the sun set on another day, if she lived that long.

"Bloody hell." Then came an even louder crash. The lock splintered and the door swung open, sending the chair flying.

Kathlyn shut her eyes and brought the poker down with all her might.

"Bloody hell," the viscount repeated when he finally regained consciousness some hours later. "I should have known you could take care of yourself." He felt the lump and gash on his head under the bandages and winced.

So did Kathlyn. Then she swiped at the tears on her cheeks so he wouldn't see how she'd been crying over his worthless body, and bristled, so he wouldn't hear how her voice still trembled. "Well, you should have identified yourself. How was I supposed to know you were not some marauder bent on wreaking havoc?"

"You should have known I'd be coming after you, blast it!"

"Of course. You needed to retrieve your property."

"What's that supposed to mean?" Deuce take it, the wretched female wasn't even glad he'd come. So much for riding *ventre-a-terre* after damsels in distress. He took a sharper look at his rescued maiden, sitting on the bed beside him. "What the devil is that you're wearing?" He tried to sit up, moaned, and fell back, still frowning dreadfully.

Kathlyn fingered the almost nonexistent neckline of the white, ruffled gown. "It's Algie's sister's. He brought it for me to wear."

"I knew I should have killed the dastard." He looked away. "Well, put a wrap over it or something, unless you're looking to get ravished."

"Here? You cannot even sit up." Still, she arranged her shawl over her shoulders, tying the ends modestly close to her throat. His lordship meanwhile muttered about how certain men would pay fortunes to defile such voluptuousness dressed in the guise of innocence.

"Are you delirious? The landlord did not think you needed a surgeon, but I could send for one."

"No, I'm not out of my mind, and you are too green by half. And what the deuce did you mean about being my property? It was no such thing, and you know it. We had an agreement, is all."

"You might believe that, and I might believe that, but no one else in the world believes that. Your friends even admitted they asked your permission to take me with them. That was bad enough, but without your nod of approval, they felt justified in absconding with me anyway, as though my wishes were of no consequence."

"I might have, ah, mentioned their lapse to them."

"You might have knocked some sense into their thick heads, but I doubt it. That's not the point. The world sees me as a fallen woman, and I cannot care for it. I do not like the way men look at me, nor the way decent women avoid looking at me. I feel soiled and unsafe, even though my conscience is clear. I did what I did for decent reasons, to help you in your, ah, difficulty, but now I cannot stay any longer. I wanted you to know that I appreciate your offer for me to remain at Mrs. Dawson's, but I can no longer pretend to be what I am not. And I wish you the best in finding a bride, although I suggest you go about it another way. Some woman will appreciate you for yourself, I'm sure, and not care so much about the other."

"What other? No, it doesn't matter. You cannot go. Where will you stay, what will you do? The pittance I gave you won't last forever."

"I shall find a respectable lodging, then look around for a suitable location for my school. London's merchant class is eager to have their daughters educated."

"Not by Gypsy whores, they're not." He reached into his pocket, trying not to move his aching head in the process, and pulled out the newspaper drawing. "Excellent likeness, don't you think?"

Kathlyn gasped, color flying into her cheeks. "Did I look like that?"

"Better, in color. The cartoon missed the red petticoats and the rose in your hair."

"Oh dear. Then I suppose I shall have to establish my young ladies' academy in Bath, or Leeds."

"What, do you think they don't receive the London journals?" Courtney shook his head, which was a mistake. He groaned, and Kathlyn hurried to put a cool cloth on his forehead. When she was finished, he took her hand. "There is another solution."

"Well, I'm not entirely sure I'll be glad to hear it, my lord, since, in hindsight, your last solution wasn't precisely needle-witted."

"You could marry me."

Kathlyn laughed. "I must be the one who is delirious. I thought you said I could marry you."

He was still holding her hand. "Kitty—Miss Partland—will you do me the great honor of becoming my wife?"

Somewhere on that soggy ride, halfway between London and Epsom, the ramifications behind Nanny's repeated revelation finally sank into Courtney's water-logged brain. Miss Kathlyn Partland was Lord Fowler's granddaughter, Lady Bellamy's niece. The implications were staggering.

He cleared his throat. "You'll have to forgive me, never done this before. That is, I did it once, but only as a formality. The arrangements were already made by our families." Courtney knew he was blathering, so he closed his eyes a moment to gather his thoughts. He missed seeing the dawning joy on her face fade to despair, the light of love shining from her remarkable eyes turn to mourning as he launched into his prepared speech.

"It has been brought to my attention that you do, indeed, have important connections among the aristocracy. You are a gently bred female of good family whose reputation, once besmirched, can never be restored except by the holy bonds of matrimony. As the, ah, instrument of your fall from grace—in the eyes of the world, if not in actuality—I am honor-bound to offer for you. You could not have foreseen the outcome of our sham affair, but I should have, being more familiar with the world of scandal and society. Therefore I take the entire responsibility for the loss of your good name by offering mine in exchange."

There, he'd gotten it out. Courtney opened his eyes again to see how his speech had been received. Not well, obviously. Kathlyn had snatched her hand from his and was busy wringing the washcloth, as if she wished it were his neck. Her chin was raised so high, he could see the pulse beating under her throat. She picked up the basin of water with murder in her flashing blue eyes, and the viscount groaned to himself. Dash it, he was barely dry from his last soaking. "Remember you're a lady."

"A lady?" she yelled, very much like a Billingsgate fishwife, but she did put down the basin, throwing the cloth in so only a little water spattered out onto the viscount's chest. "What, now I am a lady, now that I have rich relatives? Now that you know my grandfather held a prestigious title? I never even met the man, for he disowned my mother before I was born. Those other important connections you mentioned would have seen me starve in the gutter rather than lift a hand to help. No, they do not care for me, and I do not care for them."

"Fine, then we won't invite them to the wedding."

"There won't be any wedding, you gudgeon, for I am still not your property to be disposed of to fit your misguided notions of honor and propriety." She started pacing around the room. Courtney's sore head started spinning as he tried to keep her in sight. And what a sight she was, in the too tight dress and a curtain of black hair streaming down her back like a midnight waterfall. He licked suddenly dry lips. Marrying her was not going to be quite the chore he thought. Convincing her might be, though. It might take a while, but the viscount was determined to do the honorable thing. "Please, Kitty, sit down so we can talk."

"That's Miss Partland, your lordship. I am a lady, remember? I always was a lady, and in my heart I still am a lady, noble connections or not, ruined reputation or not. I have done nothing to be ashamed of. On the contrary, I feel that my actions were undertaken for the best of reasons."

"Of course they were. You had to eat. But in the eyes of society—"

"I did not play your prostitute for the money, my lord, although I'd be a fool to deny that it made the offer more palatable. And no, I did not enter into our bargain ignorant of the ways of the world. Your world. I knew precisely what would happen. What did happen, so you need not add that to your burden of guilt."

"Then why did you agree, if not for the blunt?"

Kathlyn just shook her head. He really was a blind, buffle-headed fool. If Lord Chase couldn't figure out

141

that she'd gone along with his plan because she felt sorry for him, then she couldn't tell him. She had to leave the man some pride; he had little enough else. She poured him a glass of lemonade from the pitcher by the bed. "No matter, things aren't as bad as they seem. You've forgotten that it's Kitty Parke whose reputation is ruined, not mine. That illustration might make my face too recognizable for me to set up shop in London, but my name won't be on anyone's lips. Kathlyn Partland can find a governess position in the North."

"That might have been true when we began, my dear, but I'm afraid your real name is no longer such a secret, not with Bow Street sending its hounds sniffing around Nanny's house."

"Mr. Dimm?"

"And a spotty-faced youngster puffed up with his own consequence."

"Nipperkin, oh dear."

"And it seems that Nipper—ah, Ripken informed your aunt, Lady Bellamy, that you were in Town. I'm sorry, Miss Partland, but things really are as bad as they seem. Marriage is the only solution."

"No, it's not. I could go to Canada. Marriage to you is no solution at all, it's another disaster. You don't respect me, you don't even like me half the time. And I am sorry, my lord, but I want more out of my marriage than you can offer."

He sat up, then had to grab his head with both hands lest it fall off his shoulders. "Hell and damnation, I'm one of the wealthiest men in London. You'll not do better, Miss Partland, for all your airs and graces."

Kathlyn gathered up her meager belongings and stood for a moment by the shattered door, looking at him with regret. "You poor man, if you think money is the answer to everything."

* * *

The viscount commandeered Algie's room, because it still had a lock. Algie could bunk with Woody or that tawdry blonde, Lord Chase did not care which. In the morning he commandeered their carriage. His two former friends could walk back to London, or fly. Lord Chase did not care which. Despite the raw, windy day, he sat up with the hired driver while Kathlyn rode inside to save what was left of her reputation. The viscount was suffering from concussion and inflammation of the lungs. He didn't care which carried him off first, the devil take all females.

Inspector Dimm was waiting for them in Nanny's parlor. Actually it looked to Courtney's bleary eyes as if the oldster had never left, so comfortably situated did he seem.

Nanny almost cried when she saw their condition, shrieked, "My poor baby!" and rushed toward them—to enfold Miss Partland in her ample embrace. Courtney staggered unassisted to a chair near the fire while Nanny rambled on about a hot bath and warm clothes and a soothing tisane—for Miss Partland.

Inspector Dimm did manage to pour the viscount a glass of his own brandy, from the decanter on the mantel, before he asked Miss Partland if he might have a word or two with her when she was somewhat restored.

Kathlyn agreed, on her way up the stairs with Mrs. Dawson. "But I can tell you now that I have nothing new to say except that I am sorry I was nice to Mr. Miner, I'm sorry I was nice to his lordship, and I'll never be nice to another man again!" Then she was gone.

Mr. Dimm tapped his pipe against the hearth and observed the sorry scrap of humanity sprawled on the sofa across from him. "See you did a fine job bringing the lady back all right and tight, Cap'n, and turning her up sweet. Heard you had a way with women, I did."

Lord Chase just grunted at the sarcasm from the cushioned depths.

"Want some advice from a man what was married almost three decades?"

"No, thank you," Courtney managed to croak out. "I've got the situation well in hand."

"Heard that rumor, too."

Chapter Eighteen

*W*inter had moved into Kathlyn's heart. Not the biting kind of winter, but the drab, dreary, never-ending-cold sort. It would have taken too much spirit to argue with Nanny Dawson about leaving today, and too much energy to pack, so Kathlyn stayed on. What was one more day when she had a whole eternity to plan her future—amongst untamed savages and uncivilized colonials? She misdoubted any fur-togged trapper was perishing for her to come instruct his daughter on the pianoforte. She didn't even feel like dealing with Meg's boisterous children this morning, so Nanny left Kathlyn in the parlor, curled on the sofa, a blanket and Wolfie on her knees, with her book of sonnets.

She was wondering about those odd marks when Algie and Woody arrived to ask her to marry them.

"Not both, of course, but whichever you prefer. Didn't seem right for us to decide." Since neither had thought to marry for at least a decade, they'd drawn cards. There ensued an argument whether the winner won Miss Kitty or his freedom. Hence two bruised and bloodied suitors made their singular offer for her clench-fisted hand.

Icicles dripped from Kathlyn's voice. "He sent you, didn't he?"

No need to identify who. "Not at all, Kitty, ah, Miss Parke. Told us how things stood, is all. After that it was obvious. We do know the proper thing to do, don't we, Woody?"

Woody nodded. "Gentlemen, don't you know. Our fault, bone-headed thing to do, snatching you away like we did. Need to make amends. 'Sides, it won't be all that bad. I ain't half as stuffy as old Courtney, even if I do have less than half his blunt."

"And half his looks," Algie put in. "But Courtney can't dance, and I've got all those sisters to ferry around to balls and things. You'll have fun."

Fun, being legshackled to one of the two worst widgeons she knew? She sat up straighter. "I do sincerely appreciate the offer, but—"

" 'Twould be an honor."

There was little honorable about wedding either of these two reluctant gentlemen who were already punting on tick. "You cannot want to marry me, for you both have to find wealthy brides someday."

Woody blinked his colorless lashes. "Rich chits ain't as much fun."

Kathlyn's own eyes narrowed. "I see what it is, those horses I selected won and you think to make your fortune. That's it, and his lordship's prompting, isn't it?"

Woody shook his head. "Those nags ran the way my own picks usually do, backward. And all Court said was you'd turned him down, not that we had to step into parson's mousetrap in his stead. Ain't that right, Algie?"

" 'Pon rep. 'Sides, you're a good sort of chit, Kitty, got bottom. My sisters would have had hysterics in the situation. You'll make a fine wife for some man."

"But not either of you."

Kathlyn couldn't help reflecting that her two callers looked a great deal happier leaving than they had arriving. She went back to her book.

Next to arrive was Inspector Dimm, wondering if Kathlyn had thought of anything concerning the missing jewels and warning her not to leave the house unattended in case the Miner Gang was still in the area. Since that was precisely what he'd said the night before, Kathlyn gave him directions to Meg's house, where Mrs. Dawson was spending the day. Mr. Dimm also seemed cheered to be leaving Kathlyn's company.

She had no sooner picked up her book when another knock came at the door. Wolfie didn't bother barking anymore. Lord Chase stood there, his eyes watery, his nose red and swollen, his voice raspy, as he said, "We need to talk."

"Yes, my lord, I believe we do." She led him back to the parlor and this time offered him tea.

"Then you've been thinking about my offer?"

She waved that aside. "No, I've been thinking about your condition."

"It's merely a head cold, I'm sure. The gash seems to be healing, and the lump no longer resembles an ostrich egg."

"No, no, not *that* condition. Your, ah, handicap."

He looked at the teacup balanced on his sore leg and the cane resting beside him. "I'll never win any races, but I do hope to be a creditable dancer again someday. Surely you aren't basing your decision on that?"

"My decision is final, my lord, and you are being purposely obtuse. I am speaking of the reason behind our masquerade, as you very well know. I think it is reprehensible to mislead an unsuspecting female."

Courtney set his teacup aside, no longer interested in having this conversation. He started to rise. "I believe I made it clear that my reasons were personal, none of your business."

"Oh, do sit down, my lord. I trust that I am intelligent enough to figure it out."

He sat all in a heap, trusting, nay, praying, that the other ladies of his acquaintance were as lacking in intelligence as he believed. Blast Miss Partland and her blue-stocking mind. He picked up her book of Shakespearean sonnets and flipped through it idly, trying to conceal his inner turmoil.

"Is it permanent?"

The book slipped through his fingers. "Good grief, I hope not!"

"But you aren't sure?"

"I swore my, ah, condition would end on my wedding night. I have been trying my best to keep to that promise."

That wasn't how Kathlyn understood such matters. One couldn't simply will a broken leg away, or a palsied hand. This couldn't be so dissimilar. The viscount was liable to be devastated. His *wife* was liable to be disconcerted, to say the least. Hoping to keep that poor female from such an unfortunate disappointment as a marriage in name only, without physical intimacy and without children, Kathlyn suggested, "Perhaps you should, ah, practice to be sure."

If Kitty was saying what Courtney thought she was saying, someone should wash her mouth out with soap. "I thought well-bred females didn't know about such things."

"Of course not, but having read so much, and living in the country . . . and then there was having to nurse Papa through his last illness. I suppose my education was a bit more liberal than you are used to in the ladies of your acquaintance."

"Hah!" was all he said, then he blew his nose.

Kathlyn was standing buff to her resolve. "I do not approve of your unfeeling arrogance to some innocent female on her wedding night. How could you think to wait till then to give her such a shock?"

"I *do* know the mechanics, Miss Partland. And I also read, a great deal as it happens, for that's one of the few pleasures I have allowed myself. The *Kama Sutra*, Oriental pillow books, French novels, there is a world of knowledge out there." He was so angry, his shouts were rattling the teacups. "I sincerely believe I shall not embarrass myself, Miss Partland, nor disappoint that sweet

148

young thing you are worrying about instead of your own misbegotten, misdirected, and miserable self!"

Kathlyn was dumbfounded. Could she have been so mistaken? Oh dear.

Lord Chase was on his feet now, furious. "I suppose I should thank you for rejecting my proposal, for by God, we would not suit. You'd be strangled and I'd be in prison. And thank you for turning back into the prickly hedgehog you used to be, for now I do not regret your refusal."

But Kathlyn had not been listening to his diatribe. "You mean you're not impo . . . incapa . . . unma . . ." Her mouth could not form the words.

"Bloody hell, not by half!"

"But . . . but I let you kiss me! And hold me!"

"And you seemed to enjoy yourself well enough, so what's the pother about now?"

"I thought I was safe, damn your black heart!"

"Of course you were safe, by Jupiter. What the deuce do you take me for, a ravening beast?"

"No, I took you for a eunuch, and you let me go on believing it, you dastard!" With that she tossed the cooled contents of her half-full teacup into his lap.

"Hell and damnation." He mopped at his buckskin breeches, muttering about lucky escapes, while Kathlyn fetched extra napkins.

"I do apologize, my lord, for my unseemly behavior," she said, chagrined to be acting the fishwife while professing herself a lady, a gentlewoman.

The tea seemed to have cooled the viscount's temper, too, for he was no longer shouting when he asked, "What the devil were you thinking?"

Kathlyn knew he didn't mean about throwing the tea. Studying her slippers, she said, "I thought your war injuries were, ah, of the nature to preclude any physical intimacy." All she heard back was a snort. "Well, what *was* I to think, my lord? You said you didn't have a mistress and didn't

149

want a mistress. And you never offered me carte blanche, even when you admired me."

"What, should I have? Good grief, is your pride hurt, too, besides your spinster sensibilities? I do believe you're upset that I didn't offer you a slip on the shoulder!"

"A normal man would have, especially thinking me so far beneath him socially. I suppose your admiration was as false as your war wound."

"The wound is no act, I take leave to tell you. That pistol ball was quite real. And I was attracted to you, damn it, more than I wanted to be. What did you expect me to do about it, toss you on the rug and make mad, passionate love in Nanny's parlor, just because you were dressed so provocatively in those low-cut gowns?"

" 'Twas you who dressed me like a courtesan, sirrah. Those gowns would never have been my choice."

"No, you'd have gone around in grain sacks buttoned to your throat."

"My fashion sense is not the issue; your behavior is, and I think you owe me an explanation. My reputation is ruined, I cannot show my face abroad without being recognized as a light-skirt, and I have been kidnapped by your friends." She crossed her arms over her chest and tapped her foot. "If it's not because of your injury, I want to know why."

"I have certain principles, a set of beliefs I've held my entire life."

"So do I, like 'Thou shalt not kill,' but I am seriously beginning to rethink that one. Go on."

Courtney took a deep breath. "I am a virgin."

"Excuse me?"

"You heard me, and you can shut your mouth now. Surely there are a few others around, unless we're like the unicorns that got left off the ark. I am, as trite as it may sound and as unvalued in this day and age, saving myself for marriage."

Kathlyn poured herself another cup of tea. She forgot to put in the sugar. She drank it anyway.

"We are always taught the necessity of a virgin bride," Courtney went on, "for how else is a man of worth to be assured that his heir is indeed his flesh and blood? And why should a poorer man labor to feed another man's get? Yet why isn't a husband's virtue just as important?"

Kathlyn found her voice. "Perhaps because sometimes a woman's virtue is all she has. Men have all the property and power."

"Is privilege a substitute for principle? No woman should have as her life's mate a man who has mated with half the females in England, who brings home diseases and litters the countryside with his butter stamps. It's wrong."

"That's truly what you believe, and how you live your life?" Lord Chase was such a virile man, broad-shouldered and strong-willed, Kathlyn was having trouble assimilating his words. If he'd said an evil wizard had cast a spell over him, to be broken only by the love—and marriage vows—of a good woman, she'd find it easier to accept. "You're not joking?"

"By my word, it's no laughing matter! Have you ever wanted anything so badly, your body shakes with the need? When you can't sleep, can't eat, can't think of anything but the wanting? I was not meant to be a saint, Miss Partland, for I have the same desires as every other sinner. I simply have not succumbed."

There was absolutely nothing Kathlyn could say to that. She knew Latin and Greek, French, and a bit of German. This was so far beyond her ken as to leave her reeling. The last pure male in London was sitting in Nanny's parlor, blowing his nose.

And speaking. "Unfortunately for my code of ethics, the era of chivalry has long passed. Our society, the so-called polite world, has raised licentiousness to an art form. It is considered de rigueur for a man to sport a mistress. If he's not raffish, rakish, and rumpled at four in the morning, he is not considered manly. Hence our bargain,

Miss Partland, which I can only pray you will not discuss with anyone else."

"Of course not." No one would believe it. She took another sip of the bitter tea. "Ah, not to make light of your . . . your sense of morality, but I always thought a husband should be more experienced in these things, for girls are told nothing." Kathlyn could feel herself blushing, but heavens, if he could bare his soul, she certainly could satisfy her curiosity. "You know, how it's done and all."

Courtney finally smiled. "Believe me, my dear, every boy past puberty knows how it's done."

"Oh." Kathlyn swirled the leaves around in her teacup until the warmth left her cheeks, thinking that no Gypsy fortune-teller could possibly have foreseen this happenstance. Then she set the cup aside, indicating an end to the discussion. "This is a highly improper conversation, my lord."

"Our whole relationship is highly improper, my girl, which is why we're having this talk, to try to bring some respectability to our association. I hope that, with my explanations and reflection, you've come to your senses and seen the logic of my offer."

She saw the logic—she'd always seen the logic of marrying a wealthy, well-favored viscount; she wasn't a total imbecile—but she didn't hear one word of love. And a marriage without love, well, Kathlyn had her principles, too.

Chapter Nineteen

$\mathcal{A}$ foghorn was echoing *wooo, wooo,* that melancholy, muted call into empty gray ocean. Except there was no ocean in the middle of England, no lighthouse, and no horn, only the dense winter fog and Lady Bellamy's mournful keening: "Woe, woe."

Kathlyn's aunt, traveling from Manchester to London with one lapdog, two daughters, three maids, four outriders, and five carriages, had put up at the finest inn in Leicester. There she was offered her choice of five bedrooms, four varieties of wine, three dinner menus, two private parlors, and the London newspapers, only one day old.

That could have been her sister staring out at her from the scandalous cartoon. Why, she preened, it could have been herself at an earlier age. The Bronze Age, perhaps, but there was a family resemblance. No one who saw this illustration could think the wanton so portrayed was anyone other than Gwyneth Fowler's daughter. Lady Bellamy's niece, cousin to her own precious lambs. They were ruined, ruined.

Thank heavens Lord Bellamy had decided to follow them to Town in a month, in time to pay the tradesmen and escort his wife and daughters to the opening rounds of the Season. Having made his money in the India trade and subsequently buying his title and entry into the ton, Lord Bellamy was even more conscious than his wife of the social niceties. It was not nice to have a fallen woman in one's family, not nice at all. Bellamy would have them sequestered back in Manchester before you could say jackrabbit, and then where would her girls be? Not at Almack's, that was for sure, meeting the most eligible *partis*, making the most brilliant matches.

Well, Lady Bellamy was not about to cut the offending drawing out of the paper and send it on to her spouse. She was more likely to find the offending wench and cut out her heart. No, Madorra did have some family feeling, she supposed. She'd pay the chit off and send her to the Antipodes.

But first she had to find her. She didn't doubt that Bellamy, were he in Town, could locate London's most expensive high flyer in a matter of minutes, bribe her away from her current protector, and establish her in any one of those "real estate investment properties" of his. That was decidedly not what Lady Bellamy had in mind. Nor did she wish to involve her employees in the search for her errant niece. They talked more than the gossip-mongers at afternoon teas. No, she needed someone disinterested to locate Gwyneth's girl, someone discreet. But who? Who?

Inspector Dimm wasn't happy, even though his feet were soaking in a tub of hot water and no relatives were battening on his hospitality this week. No, he wasn't happy with the way this case was going, not at all. Miss Partland wasn't any jewel thief, b'gad, and she didn't have any more knowledge of where Harry Miner stashed his booty than did Dimm's pet tabby. So the Runner wouldn't earn the reward, or his nibs's commendation. Worse, he wouldn't have any excuse to call around at Mrs. Dawson's cozy little house, not ten blocks away.

Dimm's own house was looking not as comfortable as

he'd thought, by comparison. A good cleaning, maybe new drapes, would help the shabbiness, but they wouldn't improve Dimm's cooking. He'd taken to eating his meals at coffeehouses, sitting at solitary tables with his newspaper. He always brought back some scraps so at least the cat was happy to welcome him home. Otherwise his house was very, very empty.

Well, Jeremiah Dimm hadn't given up on an investigation yet, and he wasn't going to start leaving his path strewn with unsolved cases now, like the dirty plates he seemed to forget around his house. The cat wasn't a half-bad dishwasher.

He tapped out his clay pipe and refilled it, then relit it, blowing smoke rings overhead. When a bloke reached the end of his rope, Dimm always believed, he should tie a knot and keep going. So he needed a plan, was what. If he couldn't bring in the jewels, at least he ought to be able to nab Harry's partners and Harry's murderer, especially since they were likely one and the same, the big cutpurse with the cut ear, or the smaller footpad, Sean. There was also a price on those two, nowhere near the reward Lady Bellamy was spouting for her necklace, but enough to hire a housekeeper to come in days to clean and maybe cook.

Dimm puffed on his pipe, thinking. Even the canniest rats crawled into the trap for the right bait, and Miss Kathlyn Partland was bait enough to tempt Lucifer himself out of his hidey-hole. Iffen he, Dimm, let it be known in those coffee shops and around Bow Street that he was still pursuing the chit as a lead to the jewels, the vermin would come after her, he knew it. And his plan wouldn't be jeopardizing Miss Partland at all, he reasoned, because he'd have Nipperkin stationed across the street watching. Of course, Bow Street's finest would be right there to guard her every minute, too, right where he wanted to be, at Mrs. Dawson's. Those two sneak thieves might as well be fitted for hempen neckties.

* * *

"I say we go north and search again, Quig. Harry must of stashed the rocks afore he ever got on that coach."

"What, the fifteen miles between where you stabbed him and where he caught the Mail? We been there, Sean. The Runners've been there. Harry stole a horse, too, remember? He could of put the bundle in the fork of a tree, for all we know. Know how many trees there are between two postin' inns? 'Sides, half of 'em are under snow."

"Shut up, both of you. I say we go after the girl. You should have seen the way her man lit into his friends at Epsom. I wish I'd had blunt on the match. He'll come down heavy to get her back, I know it."

"But kidnappin', Ursula? We ain't never been in that line." Quigley scratched his armpit.

"We ain't never been in Newgate either, but that's where we're headed if you bunglers keep trying to snatch reticules off old ladies." She frowned over at Quigley, who was too busy itching to notice, nor the way she kept her distance. "Else you two incompetents'll be laid in the ground somewheres."

"How'd I know she had a pistol in her purse?" Sean whined. Now part was missing from his ear, too.

Ursula pinched her cheeks. It was cheaper than rouge. "No, the girl's our only chance to make a killing."

"You said no killin'."

"What, you're getting religion on us, Quigley? It never stopped you from shooting that guard or Petey."

"He weren't a female. I don't cotton to hurtin' females."

Ursula filed that away for future reference, but for now she told her cohorts, "We won't hurt a hair on her head. Well, maybe cut off a snip or two to send the viscount so he knows we've got his little dove. He'll come running with the gold, the same as he came running to Epsom after her. You'd think he was married to the chit or something."

* * *

"Oh, my word, what if he marries her?" Rosemary, Viscountess Chase, shredded her handkerchief as she sat in the pretty morning room of her rented house in Trowbridge. In front of her were three letters from faithful correspondents and three, count them, three copies of that wretched cartoon. The drawing was bad enough, showing a female of unmistakable appeal—at least her son had good taste—but the letters were worse. He was taking the female to museums, by heaven! A gentleman took his mistress to the park, the theater, anywhere he could show her off, not to museums and monuments! 'Twas almost as if Courtney thought the baggage had something beside feathers between her ears. Worst of all, dear Lord, he was defending her.

Her son was defending a Covent Garden convenient! Lady Chase knew the boy, knew Courtney didn't take these things lightly. Not for him any mindless tumble with a bit of nameless fluff, oh, no. He had to go find himself a woman of wit and wounded sensibilities, then put her on a pedestal for others to admire, and him to protect. The quixotic clunch must have gone and fallen in love with his mistress.

Drat him for not being infatuated with the gardener's daughter when he was sixteen, his tutor's wife when he was seventeen, Harriet Wilson and her sisters when he came on the Town. He'd be long over such calf-love catastrophes. But no, he was too serious as a young man, too responsible, too aware of what he owed his name and dignity, which traits he definitely had not inherited from his father, the libertine. Not that Lady Chase would prefer her son to be a profligate womanizer; she only wished he'd gone wading more, before jumping in over his head.

What if he married the jade? It would be the misalliance of the century, that's what. They'd never be received and her grandchildren would be taunted by bullies. She'd never be able to show her face in Town, perhaps not even in Bath where Reverend Hollingsworth was a particular friend of hers, not with such a daughter-in-law.

Lady Chase tried to reread the letters, but they were too streaked and sodden with her tears. There was nothing for it but to order her things packed, to go put an end to this affair herself. Courtney was a good boy; he'd always listened to his mama. If not, she'd just have to buy off the mercenary miss.

Lady Chase didn't blame the gel, not in the least. She blamed that snippety Adelina Marlowe for jilting her dearest boy and giving him a disgust of decent women-folk. Why, if he'd married that flighty baggage, he could maintain five mistresses with the ton's blessings—and his mother's.

So he wasn't a blessed monk after all, Adelina fumed, glaring at the latest *on dits* column from a reporter who had been in Epsom for the races. That dastard. Not the reporter, the scoundrel who'd fed her a bushel of hog swill so he could weasel out of their betrothal.

Adelina could have been a viscountess, damn his eyes. She hurled a china shepherdess across the room.

"What, my love, did you drop something?" her husband asked. Her old, scaly-skinned, foul-breathed maggot of a minor lordling husband. A china milkmaid followed her sister to porcelain purgatory. If not for that craven Courtney and his garish girlfriend, Adelina could have been a duchess someday.

The Duke of Caswell rubbed his gnarled hands in glee. Why, this was a new lease on life, news to warm the cockles of an old man's heart. His heir, his only grand-son, actually had some wild oats to sow.

His Grace treated himself to a glass of port to cele-brate, doctor's orders be damned. Maybe he'd even toddle off to Town and take a look at Chase's high flyer for himself. Any female enticing enough to light a fire under that prig Courtney ought to be able to breathe some life into Caswell's fading embers. He'd give the boy a run for his money, see if he didn't.

* * *

Courtney's nose was running, his head was stuffed, and his temper was as frayed as the skin on his knuckles. He didn't want to check on his gelding's foreleg; he didn't want to meet with his solicitor; he didn't want to sit at his blasted club and listen to the gossip. He dashed well knew he *was* the latest gossip. Thunderation, how did this happen to him? All he'd done was bring some pitiful waif in out of the cold. He'd have done as much for any stray. Now his name took up a whole page in White's betting book, and he had to go quiet the rumors—or bash a few more heads together.

What he wanted to do was stay at home nursing his cold, his manly pride, and a grudge against independent-thinking females. By George, he did know what was best for the chit.

And just possibly what was best for him, too.

And Kathlyn Partland, the focus of more interest than she'd known her entire life? She was upstairs at Nanny's, nursing a broken heart.

Chapter Twenty

No snow, no rain, no fog—and no excuse not to leave London. Soon 'twould be the season of new growth, and Kathlyn had to start her new life. So far she couldn't decide if she wanted to speak to land agents about a school in the far north of England, or booking agents about passage to the Colonies. The only decision she'd managed to make was an easy one: she had to leave. Lord Chase could stop feeling so conscience-stricken, Nanny could stop muttering about fools who couldn't see the noses on their faces, and Kathlyn could stop wishing for the moon. She had to leave shortly, too, before she lied herself into believing that the moon was in reach.

Someone else couldn't wait for spring's resurgence. Meg's baby decided to arrive a month ahead of schedule, cold weather or no. The midwife predicted a difficult birth, Nanny was frantic, Meg's children were distraught. Kathlyn couldn't think of her own problems at a time like this. She couldn't think of leaving while she was so needed.

The screaming, crying, and wailing were something fierce—and that was just Meg's husband, Jonathan.

"Send for Master Courtney," Nanny directed. "He'll get the ninny calmed down."

"What, Lord Chase? You cannot mean the viscount to be here at a time like this," Kathlyn said with pleading in her voice. "Meg wouldn't want to see his lordship." What Kathlyn meant was, she didn't want to see him.

"Gammon, they're like brother and sister. Raised on the same mother's milk, weren't they? He'd ought to be here, and Jonathan needs the diversion. And the children adore him, of course. Their godfather, don't you know."

His toplofty lordship standing godfather to two bank clerk's babes? Kathlyn wasn't even surprised anymore at anything she learned about the man. She was wondering if she should send Lizzie with the message—Little George could accompany her—or try to find a boy in the street to carry Nanny's request.

"I'll send Nipperkin. Give the sprig something to do." Inspector Dimm had invited himself along to Meg's, saying he'd been through so many birthings, he could likely stand in for the midwife. "Had to once, in an emergency. Might be handy to have around."

Kathlyn allowed as though he might be, if only to keep Jonathan from drinking alone. But what was Ripken doing in the neighborhood? Inspector Dimm had become a fixture at Nanny's, but Ripken had been least in sight, which pleased Kathlyn as much as her private suspicions concerning the inspector's presence. She simply couldn't like the brash young Runner, remembering how he'd accused her of any number of nefarious deeds. "I thought your assistant was off looking for Mr. Miner's associates."

Dimm needed to polish his spectacles. "Well, I thought it might be a good idea for him to keep an eye out around here, in case the gang still thinks Harry told you something."

"Bosh, they couldn't still believe that poppycock, not after all this time."

They could, if Inspector Dimm told them. He'd spread the word in the coffee shops and at Bow Street that he wasn't convinced of the female's innocence, just couldn't prove her guilt. And he'd gone to the park a few times, taking his sweet roll and a sack of peanuts. Sure enough, that dark-haired widow in the heavy veil came to sit beside him. He noted that she didn't have any peanuts with her.

"Why, Inspector Dimm, what a surprise. I thought you'd left town."

"No, ma'am. Working hard to crack the case I'm working on. That jewel theft, don't you know."

"Did you solve it, then?"

"No, but I'm close. I'll have my hands on those sparklers and the reward money within the sennight."

"Oh, then you know where they are?"

"No, but I know who does."

Now Dimm couldn't quite meet Miss Partland's eyes as he told her she was right, that there was likely nothing to worry about except seeing Meg's baby birthed. Ripken just had nothing better to do.

That's what he told the viscount, too, when his lord-ship appeared. Courtney was pleased that extra measures were being taken to protect Miss Partland's safety, even if they were unnecessary. One Runner was a precaution, two were a superfluity, except that Ripken knew how to play whist. Playing for pennies, they managed to keep Jonathan's mind occupied for the next day and night. Courtney even could ignore Miss Partland's presence for an entire hour at a stretch, when she wasn't bustling in and out of Meg's bedchamber or fussing over the children.

Approximately two eternities later they heard a tiny wail. Kathlyn came out and announced, "Jonathan, you have another son. A beautiful, tiny boy. Meg is tired, but the midwife promises she'll make a good recovery."

Some time later, during which the men toasted the new arrival, his clever mother, the midwife, the king, and the Duke of Wellington, among others, they were all per-mitted in to see Meg and her son.

Jonathan sat next to Meg on the bed, his daughter in his arms so she could see the new baby. The older boy sat on Meg's other side, exclaiming over the infant's minuscule fingers and toes. Nanny was beaming, wiping tears of happiness from her eyes, and Inspector Dimm was patting her on the shoulder. "I told you there was nothing to it." Ripken had declined the invitation to the birthing room, turning so red in the face that his spotted complexion didn't show, for once.

After hugs and congratulations, Kathlyn and Courtney both moved to the doorway, to give the family more space. Together they gazed back fondly at the scene.

So much love shone in the room, so much joy and contentment, that their stares became almost envious. This is what I want, Kathlyn thought, this kind of love.

This is what I want in my marriage, Courtney thought, this kind of love.

Suddenly aware of how close they stood, and embarrassed that the other might guess their thoughts, the viscount and Kathlyn sprang apart, she to fix tea, and Courtney to help Ripken pack away the cards and the deal table.

Meg was recovering, but slowly. Kathlyn felt she couldn't leave yet, not with Jonathan back to work at the bank and Nanny taking charge of the fussy infant so Meg could get some rest. The other children tried to help, but they needed attention, too, and someone to play with them. Their lessons were more crucial now also, especially for Meg's older boy, Philip, because the viscount had offered to send the bright child to school next year if he passed the entrance examinations.

Kathlyn was happy enough to spend her free hours refurbishing her wardrobe again, this time trying to make the viscount's purchases less stylish, more suitable for a spinster lady seeking employment than for a strumpet. She filled in a neckline here and removed some trimming there. There was nothing she could do—

or wanted to do, truth be told—about the rich fabrics, the silks and sheer muslins, except learn to knit shawls with Nanny's instructions. Other times she read aloud to Nanny and Meg, from the Minerva Press novels they both clucked their tongues over, and begged for more. They weren't interested in Shakespeare at all, although Kathlyn toted her book of sonnets around in her cloak pocket just in case.

Lord Chase stayed away for the most part, to Kathlyn's relief. She thought he was being thoughtful of her feelings and the awkwardness that had come between them. He thought he looked absurd with a head cold, with his nose all red and swollen, so he waited to feel better, and for a slightly warmer day.

"A drive in the park? How delightful. The children will love it."

Courtney didn't recall inviting the children, but he wasn't to be outmaneuvered. Two loaves of bread and an admonition to Philip to watch his sister saw them happily feeding the ducks along the Serpentine, in sight but out of hearing.

"You truly like children, Miss Partland." It was a statement, not a question.

"Why, yes, I do, especially these two. I noticed you are quite fond of them yourself, although I do recall that you turned down Meg's offer to hold the new baby."

"I still have a touch of the cold, don't you know," he said, excusing his cowardice. That infant was the smallest, most fragile-looking bit of humanity he'd ever seen. And it cried. He cleared his throat. "Ahem. What I am trying to get at is that I can give you children, you know."

Oh dear, was he never going to forget her horrid misconception? She'd have a permanent blush. "My lord, I do understand that if one can, ah, fulfill one's marital duties, then babies are the natural outcome. Contrary to your estimations of my innocence or intelligence, I did not think that children were found under cabbage leaves!"

"That wasn't what I meant, dash it." Thunderation, now he'd gotten her riled up again, although with Miss Partland that was no rare occurrence. Stalling, Courtney tightened his muffler around his neck. "Are you warm enough?"

The one garment she wouldn't alter, wouldn't regret, was the fur-lined blue pelisse. "Yes, thank you, my lord, quite warm."

"Deuce take it, do you think we can dispense with the 'my lords' and 'misses'? Please, I beg you to make free with Courtney, Chase, or Choate, whichever you prefer. Given the nature of our relationship, titles are absurd."

"Given the nature of our relationship—noble employer, former employee—titles are a necessity, my lord," Kathlyn countered, but she did relent and say, "You may call me Kitty, however, for people would think it odd if you did not."

"It only suits you when you smile," he mumbled into his muffler.

"Pardon? Perhaps we should return home now, if you are still ailing. You wouldn't want your throat to turn putrid."

As putrid as his mood had been the last week. "Botheration, Kath—Kitty, I'm trying to ask you to consider my offer again. I know we've been round Robin's barn about your reputation and my obligation to restore it, and you cannot be blind to the material advantages I can provide: money, property, social standing. I know you're not mercenary—did I mention there were four houses and the hunting box?—or mad to acquire a title, although I don't know another woman who wouldn't sell her soul to be a duchess one day. For that matter, I don't know another man who can promise fidelity with such sincerity. That's all been said, though. I thought I'd try a new tack."

"And I thought we'd agreed to consider the discussion closed." Kathlyn turned toward the carriage, but he took her arm and headed back to the waterside.

"A good soldier knows when to retreat to fight another

day. But truly, Kitty, I believe that once you've considered all the advantages, you'll come to my way of thinking." To Courtney's thinking, this stubborn wench did not belong out of his sight, much less out of his life. He'd been wanting to get married. He'd been wanting to end his self-imposed restraint, and by Jupiter, he'd been wanting this particular female with every fiber of his being.

He couldn't come out and say that he dreamed of touching her every night, that he wanted to worship every inch of her perfect body, that he wanted to lose himself in her silky tenderness. She'd run screaming to New South Wales, which was what he'd be doing soon if she didn't agree to marry him.

"So I thought I'd remind you about the children, your own children, not some runny-nosed school-yard brats."

"What, and your progeny wouldn't have runny noses?" she asked, pointedly staring at his own slightly patrician prominence.

Courtney pulled out a handkerchief. "Of course not, they'll be perfect angels." He could visualize dark-haired cherubs playing at her skirts.

Kathlyn pictured a little boy with golden ringlets—and a red nose. No, she would not let him do this, this melting of her resolve. Snow might give way to thawing temperatures, but the ice fortress around her heart had to be made of sterner stuff.

Courtney Chase was everything a woman could want in a husband: a good provider, a doting parent, a devoted partner. He was, in fact and in misfortune, the only man Kathlyn could want for a husband. He wasn't haughty and arrogant; he was honorable and ethical, a man she would gladly trust with her life—but not her heart. He'd do his damnedest to see her wed to him because his honor demanded it—but not his heart.

He'd be a faithful husband, Kathlyn had no doubt, until he fell in love with a woman of his own milieu, one who was welcome in the Queen's Drawing Room, who could run a ducal mansion, and whose children never had dirty faces. Then he'd still be a dutiful husband because he was such an honorable man, but he'd be miserable. Kathlyn loved him too much to do that to him, or to herself.

"No, my lord, I fear that if you want to give me children, you shall have to find yourself a wellborn bride, beget yourself a parcel of perfect poppets, and send them to my school."

Chapter Twenty-one

$\mathcal{W}$inter was hanging on like an old dog with nubby teeth. He'd slink off in the end, but not before giving the enemy something to remember.

A bitter wind swept across the land, not bothering with snow or rain, just making people wretched enough with the icy gale. The temperatures dropped and dropped and dropped until washing hung outside turned to rigid banners, wells wouldn't pump, and horses' breaths froze into ice packs around their muzzles. Newspapers, when they were thawed out enough to open, warned of frostbite, lung damage, and possible death by congealing blood. Parties were canceled, shops were closed, and even London's beggars were forced off the streets. The only ones doing any business were the icemen, out and about cutting blocks of ice to store belowground for summer use; they sure as Hades weren't selling any now.

Lady Chase's coachman in Trowbridge flatly refused to set out in such weather. The viscount would have his head for sure, imperiling his lordship's prime cattle, to say nothing of his lordship's mother. So Lady Chase kept searching the newspapers, dreading to find her son's name.

Lady Bellamy was nearly to London, stalled at an inn by the iced-over roads, though one more day of her daughters' brangling would see her hiring a sled to convey them the last few stages. At least the inn received the London papers, a mere few hours off the presses, although the delivery boy had to be pried off his horse. Lady Bellamy kept scanning the slander sheets, dreading to find her niece's name.

The Duke of Caswell didn't wait for the London journals; he had a whole network of secretaries, solicitors, and servants doing his spying for him so he could stay warm and comfortable, at home.

Harry Miner's gang took to burning newspapers, when they could find them, for their meager heat. Unfortunately for Ursula, not even ladies in her profession could ply their trade in this cold, so she was forced to let Sean and Quigley move into her Chelsea rooms to pool their resources. Even more unfortunately for Ursula, the erstwhile thieves packed their parasites along, too. When it came to arguing, the spoiled Bellamy siblings had nothing on three failed felons in a flea-ridden flat.

"I say if she don't show her nose soon, we break into the house and snatch her away."

"What, under the eye of that old Runner what's practically moved in there to protect the mort? 'Sides, there's the dog and the dummy."

"Well, she has the young'un trailin' her skirts when she does leave the house to go to t'other place, so it's seven of one, half a dozen of t'other."

"He's a boy, ain't he?" asked Ursula. "Don't worry about the sprat. I'll take care of him."

So they went back to arguing over whose turn it was to go out for bread—and itching powder.

After three or four days, mongrel winter loosened its grip on the city. People could move about again, if they were careful of the icy patches and didn't stand in one place too long. Travelers could continue their journeys, tradesmen could hawk their wares. The only one not happy with the chance to be out-of-doors again was

Inspector Dimm, for now he had to report to his superior about the failure of his plan.

" 'Twere a good plan, too, if not for that jackanapes Ripken," Mr. Dimm told his cat. "A'course, I couldn't say that to the governor, him being the Nipperkin's kin and all."

The young Runner had decided that if Miss Partland wasn't guilty, then she was a goddess. "Gorblimey, the lackwit's tossed his hat over the windmill for sure. If 'is nibs thinks he's aggravated with me not finding the jewels, I can't wait till he hears about me losing his nevvy to a female what's blotted her copybook."

Dimm didn't believe Miss Partland was a sneak thief, a light-skirt, or liable to lead that chub Ripken astray. Why, the cawker was so tongued-tied in her presence now, she likely was not aware of his silent adoration. She had to be aware, though, of Ripken's dogging her foot-steps since he was hardly ever more than a foot away. "To keep her safe," the clunch explained. More like to get a whiff of her perfume, or a glimpse of skin, or a not-so-accidental touch when he held the door open for her. Dimm shook his head. The mooncalf never stood a chance of winning more than a polite smile, not when it was as plain as a pimple on the peabrain's nose that the lady had eyes for no one but the viscount. Heaven alone knew how that situation was going to unfold, for heaven alone could figure out the workings of a woman's mind. Meantime his lordship was making micefeet of his courting, and more to the point, Ripken was scaring away the jewel thieves.

Even a half-weaned hound can deter trespassers, albeit just by setting up a howl. No one looking at Ripken would cringe in terror, but no would-be kidnappers would want him looking their way, either.

So Dimm revised his strategy. Telling Miss Partland the danger was likely passed after all this time, he let her go unaccompanied back and forth to Meg's house, sta-tioning Ripken out of sight down the alley across the street. B'gad, he thought, maybe standing out in the cold would cool the jackass's ardor. Dimm, naturally, would continue his vigil, too, from right there in Mrs. Dawson's parlor window. The new plan ought to keep the governor from complaining, if not content. It sure made Mr. Dimm happy.

Happiest of all with the moderating temperatures were the children, who could finally go out to play, unless it was Kathlyn, who'd been cooped up with their boundless energy for ages, it seemed. Or perhaps his lordship was most pleased, for now he had an excuse to call on Miss Partland, to invite her and the children to go skating.

No, Harry's gang was happiest to see her outside more, for they were close to burning the furniture for firewood.

"Yeah, but now she's lost the Runner runt, she's got the toff totin' her ice skates," Sean whined.

Quigley bashed him on his good ear. "That means he loves her, you cabbage-head. An' the chummier them two get, the more he'll pay to get her back onct we nab her. 'Sides, they can't be ice-skating forever."

They could skate for hours every day, however, despite the cold and despite the viscount's weak leg. Courtney's wound seemed to improve with the exercise on the frozen ornamental lakes in the park as they laughed and played, instructed the children, and performed magical ice dances. When they grew tired or cold or his leg finally gave out, they all went to Gunther's, tearooms, or chocolate shops. And they didn't only go skating. They went to the circus and the menagerie and the waxworks museum. Courtney made sure that Kathlyn couldn't refuse, for the children's sakes. Like Mr. Dimm, the viscount had a plan.

Kathlyn was going to become his wife. That was a fact, in his heart and in his mind, if not in his immediate future. It wasn't merely a matter of satisfying his honor anymore, to save her from an ignominious reputation;

now it was a matter of fulfilling his dreams. He couldn't even recall wanting a demure little debutante bride, all simpers and spit curls. What would he speak of to a nursery-fresh ninny? How could he argue about the Corn Laws and enclosures with a chit more knowledgeable of fashions and the latest gossip? Besides, how could he take another female to wife when all he wanted was Kathlyn Partland? That would be counter to his lifelong tenets. He, of all men, would finally make love to a woman, only to be having adulterous thoughts of another! Why, he'd have saved his body for his bride, only to have his mind unfaithful. To even contemplate such a circumstance was absurd! He'd have Kathlyn or no other.

She was in his dreams, waking and sleeping. When they were out abroad, he'd dream what he'd do with her abed. When he was home alone in his huge four-poster, he suffered. Oh, how he suffered. Kathlyn was beautiful and bright, spirited and sensitive, proud—and pure. She was everything he wanted. They'd have a good life together, if only he could convince the stubborn little shrew.

Well, Courtney was stubborn, too. He'd kept a difficult—no, a well-nigh impossible—vow all these years; he could outlast any mulish miss. Bribery didn't work, appeals to logic had availed him nothing, and citing her lost reputation only reminded her what a nodcock he could be. So now he had a new plan. He was going to make Kathlyn love him, by George!

First she had to like him, so he'd show her what a friendly chap he could be, likable, easygoing, a good companion. He wouldn't even threaten to strangle her if she mentioned emigrating to Canada again. Since she was as skittish as a colt around him, he made sure the children were present, just as he made sure she couldn't refuse his invitations without disappointing his godchildren. He did have a modicum of intelligence, despite Inspector Dimm's opinion.

The opinion around Town varied, depending on the quarter from which it came.

The children were too old to be Kitty Parke's, everyone agreed. Everyone who saw her, that was, which was nearly everyone returned to Town by the time the ice melted. His lordship had no nieces or nephews or young cousins, the gossips concurred, yet he appeared to dote on these two youngsters.

"Must be that Mrs. Dawson's," Algie confided to his friend.

Woody looked around at the crowded tables at White's, then back at the betting book. He gingerly touched the bandage across his broken nose. "We weren't supposed to talk about any of them, remember?"

Algie lowered his voice, easy with his recently dislocated jaw. "Deuce take it, everyone else in London is. What did the gudgeon expect, when he parades his mistress and two by-blows around Town? Lud, we may as well make some blunt off the wagering."

So the rumor mills ground on: Viscount Chase had two mistresses, two illegitimate children, in two houses in Kensington. His own dear friends, the ones who'd helped him fend off the footpads in Epsom, poor brave things, practically confirmed it.

The old duke slapped his thigh and nearly fell over laughing. Damn if the boy didn't have cullions after all! And damn, but that was one accommodating mistress the lad had found for himself, taking on another whore's whelps. Now, if Chase would only find a wellborn bride half so obliging, His Grace could finally stop worrying over the succession. The duke admitted that the cub had been wise to end that engagement he'd encouraged so hard, for the Marlowe chit wouldn't have known the first thing about satisfying such a lustful lad, bless his fruitful soul.

Two mistresses, the cad had? Two children while he was spouting about virtue and the sanctity of the marriage

173

bed? Lady Fostwick, née Adelina Marlowe, smashed two of Lord Fostwick's favorite snuffboxes against the wall. Now the drawing room smelled as bad as the old goat she was married to.

She'd been married to a rake, and she'd given birth to a rake. It was too, too much for Lady Chase to bear, so she took to her bed at Choate House in Grosvenor Square and refused to come out until she ran out of hand-kerchiefs to dry her eyes. She had her maid tell Courtney she was ill from the journey to Town.

She was sick, all right, sick with knowing she'd failed to instill the least bit of decency in her philandering hus-band's son. And she'd tried so hard to make Courtney a better man than that dirty dish who'd sired him, likely when Chase was between mistresses. What was she going to tell Reverend Hollingsworth? Oh, children were the very devil.

That devil and his doxy were trying to ruin her chil-dren's lives! It was scandalous enough that Gwyneth's girl was a member of the muslin company, but a *ménage à trois*? Lady Bellamy heard of nothing else at the modistes' and the morning calls, over tea or over the latest tenor. All of London was abuzz with the most recent scandal. The only thing she didn't hear, thank heaven and all the stars that shone in it, was this Kitty Parke's real name. No one was exclaiming over her simi-larity to Lady Bellamy or her deceased sister. Yet. Most likely the gabble-grinders were too busy inspecting those children for a resemblance to his libertine lordship to notice anything else. Yet.

They'd be ruined. Lord Bellamy would be furious. First she'd lost her diamonds, now she'd lose their entrée to the haut monde. Her only hope was to get rid of the girl before her identity came out. But how? By all reports the chit was having a high old time of it, so it would take a fortune to buy her off.

On that long journey to Town Lady Bellamy had conceded that she knew only one man who could possibly handle the delicate negotiations, besides finding the wayward wench in the first place. He'd be discreet and understanding, having daughters himself, even if he wasn't the cleverest detective on Bow Street's staff.

As he read Lady Bellamy's carefully worded note, Inspector Dimm decided this was going to be the easiest money he ever earned, reuniting aunt and niece. Besides, Mrs. Dawson would be pleased as punch to see her protégé back in the bosom of her niffy-naffy family instead of going out as a governess or such. 'Twould give that chaw-bacon Lord Chase a nudge, too, to see Miss Partland taking her place in society.

Kathlyn set the places for supper, smiling. He liked her. Lord Chase didn't have to spend so much time with her; he could take the children places on his own if he wished. He could leave them altogether and go back to his own world. But he didn't. He liked skating and sightseeing and strawberry tarts. And he liked her. Maybe Canada wasn't such a good idea. She heard it was cold.

Chapter Twenty-two

The sun was out. Like Kathlyn's old cape that she'd worn to London, it was thin and threadbare, ragged around the edges, and did not provide much warmth, but the sun was out at last.

Kathlyn still wore her new fur-lined pelisse instead of a short spencer, because Nanny insisted that there was nothing more dangerous than rushing the warm weather. Kathlyn kissed the older woman's rounded cheek, laughing. "What would I do without you to worry over me, dear Mrs. Dawson?"

Handing her a covered basket, Nanny smiled and said, "Get on with you, dearie. Spanish coin won't get you any more of my raspberry tarts, nor turn me up sweet after you sent Lizzie on home."

"But her mother was ill, and I'm only going to Meg's house, you know."

"That's as may be, but a lady never steps out of her house without escort." Before Kathlyn could protest once more that she was no such rarefied being, only a humble governess, Nanny went on. "Shoo, now, go. The children will be wondering what happened to their lessons."

"Oh, they'll never settle to their books today, not with the picnic to Richmond this afternoon. They'll be looking out the window for his lordship's carriage all morning."

"And I suppose you won't be, eh?" Nanny teased, and Kathlyn pretended indifference, commanding her feet not to race out the door and skip down the street. She turned and waved good-bye to Mr. Dimm, who'd come for breakfast as was his wont lately, along with midday dinner and late tea. Standing in the window, he waved his pipe and smiled.

Mr. Dimm seemed mightily pleased about that mysterious private business he was transacting this morning, Kathlyn thought. Or else he was in love, too. Wouldn't that be wonderful? She swung her basket in sheer exuberance—because the sun was finally shining, she told herself—and even gave a gay wave to young Master Ripken down that alley where he thought he was in concealment.

Dimm stood by the window, finishing his pipe before he left for his interview with Lady Bellamy. He watched Miss Partland dance down the street and wave to that rattlepate Ripken, deciding that seeing the chit claimed by her kin was going to be better than finding the diamonds. Something out of a fairy tale, it was, with a handsome prince and all, or the next best thing. Better, considering the state of Prinny's pocketbook. And he, Jeremiah Dimm, was getting to play fairy godfather. He nodded. Too bad about the diamonds, though.

The Runner put on his coat and gloves and accepted a raspberry tart wrapped in linen from Mrs. Dawson. Dimm allowed as how he ought to remember to bring a bouquet of flowers back with him, to celebrate. Females set a great store by such things, b'gad.

As he left he noticed a woman walk down Ripken's alley. She had red hair under her bonnet, and a black wrap. Dimm couldn't recognize her—not at this distance, even with his spectacles—but something about her looked familiar. He shrugged and went in the other direction. Most likely a neighbor lady, he figured. No matter,

Ripken would keep an eye on Miss Partland, two if he knew what was good for him.

Kathlyn was humming as she turned the corner onto Meg's street. What a lovely morning!

"No, I'm sorry, but I don't know of any Hand Street," she told the driver of the ramshackle coach pulled alongside the curb there. He had his hat pulled so low over his forehead that he most likely couldn't read the street signs, or perhaps he couldn't read at all. "I haven't been in the neighborhood for very—"

Before Kathlyn could complete the sentence, something shoved her from behind so hard that only her outstretched arms kept her head from banging into the carriage. "What—"

Strong hands grabbed her shoulders, pulling her hood up over her face and pushing her into the coach, which immediately took off at a great rate of speed, swaying as her attacker leaped aboard.

Kathlyn took a moment to catch her breath and uncover her eyes, then she took stock of the situation. The curtains were nailed over the windows, and the doors were locked from the outside. Yes, this had all the trappings of an abduction.

Courtney would kill them this time, Kathlyn feared, calmly setting herself to rights. And she'd have a few choice words for Algie and Woody herself. She couldn't imagine what they wanted with her now, or where they were taking her, only that a wager was involved. Oh, she'd give those two basket scramblers a rare trimming, she would. She might even permit the viscount to frighten them a bit, to teach them not to terrorize innocent victims. Not that she was afraid or anything, Kathlyn assured herself. It was simply that she had a niggling doubt about Woody driving such sorry nags as the breakdowns hitched to this carriage, and a teensy misgiving about Algie ever smelling as bad as the man who pushed her.

When the carriage halted some time later, the door was

pulled open, but a blanket was thrown over Kathlyn before her eyes could adjust to the brighter light.

"Put me down, you cockleheads. Someone will see you and call the Watch. You'll get arrested before Courtney gets his chance at you."

Not only were her words so muffled by the heavy fabric that they were almost unintelligible, but her abductors didn't care. They were two men carrying a rolled carpet between them, which was unexceptional in this neighborhood where no one asked a lot of questions anyway.

"Woody? Algie?" No answer. No way Lord Chase's friends would have treated any female so recklessly, either. Kathlyn was forced to admit that she had, in fact, been abducted. The carpet muffled her panicked screams.

Dumped out onto a hard mattress, Kathlyn instantly clamped her hands over her eyes. "No, I won't look. I mustn't see you."

"Ursie never told us she was attics to let, Quig."

Kathlyn kept her eyes covered. "I know, you'll kill me if I can identify you."

Sean just stood scratching his head, but Quigley asked, "What do we care? We already got our phizzes on wanted posters, and they can't hang us twice."

" 'Sides, soon as we get the blunt, we're goin' to Canada. Make a new life for us there. We hear they don't have but one guard watchin' the mail coaches."

Which was another reason Kathlyn was glad she'd decided against Canada.

"And we got to talk, missy." Quigley gingerly nudged her shoulder.

So Kathlyn took her hands away and looked, then almost screamed again. One of her kidnappers was tall, the other short, but both men were ill dressed and filthy, and both had parts of their ears missing, as if there were some odd initiation into the criminal class. But Kathlyn knew those faces. She'd seen those posters.

"Why, you're Mr. Miner's associates."

Quigley cuffed at Sean. "There, knew she was a downy bird. And don't it sound pretty, 'Mr. Miner's associates?' "

"It'd sound prettier still, Quig, if missy was to tell us what Harry had to say." They both looked at her expectantly.

Kathlyn shook her head, brushing back her hair that had come loose from its coils. "I'm sorry that you went to all this trouble for nothing, sirs. If I knew anything at all, I would have told Bow Street. We'll all pretend this never happened, shall we? I'll be going, if you'll open the door."

The door opened, but a woman entered the little room. Kathlyn knew her, too, from the Argyle Rooms and from Epsom. "Why, you've been following me all along, haven't you?" Kathlyn gasped.

"And no picnic, either, ducks." Ursula hungrily eyed the basket that had miraculously stayed hooked over Kathlyn's arm. "So make it worth our while and tell us where Harry hid the diamonds."

"I was telling these, ah, gentlemen that Mr. Miner didn't tell me anything. He kindly thanked me for bringing him some food and drink, and then he died."

Ursula sniffed and wiped at her eyes with her sleeve. "Wasn't that just like old Harry, going off like a gent. He always did know how to act like a posh swell, didn't he, boys?"

The others nodded, averting their eyes for a moment in respect for the man they'd killed. "A regular flash cove, our Harry."

The smaller felon added for Kathlyn's benefit, "That's how we did so good at the thieving ken. Harry passed hisself off as a guest at them nobs' dos, then made off with the goods when no one was looking."

That was more information than Kathlyn thought she needed to know right now. "I, ah, see. But now that Mr. Miner has, ah, gone aloft"—if that's where courtly jewel thieves went, although she highly doubted it, if there was any justice in this world, or the next—"there is nothing more I can do. He never mentioned a word about diamonds, stealing anything, or hiding anything." He had mentioned something about Kathlyn getting a reward for her kindness, now that she recalled, but she'd thought he was being grateful, not literal. She didn't think she'd mention her latest memory to this audience.

Ursula must have seen the sudden light of comprehension in Kathlyn's eyes, for she demanded, "He said something else, didn't he? You're holding something back, I know it."

"Mr. Miner, ah, said he'd miss his wife," she prevaricated. "I wasn't sure if I should mention it, not knowing if you were she."

"He never did," Ursula cooed. After she turned him in and all? "That was my Harry, all right, a real sport." She dabbed at her eyes a bit more, then turned to the men. "Let's get on with it."

"But I told you, I don't know anything important."

"But you do know someone important, ducks. Someone who'll pay a king's ransom to get you back."

Courtney, of course. Kathlyn couldn't let him get involved, not with these ragged ruffians. "No, there's no one. Only old Mrs. Dawson, and you've seen where she lives. She couldn't pay your way to Cornwall, much less Canada."

"Nice try, ducks, but we know about your fancy man."

"He's not—"

Kathlyn might as well have saved her breath, for Ursula turned to Sean. "Get the scissors."

Oh, no! Kathlyn slapped her hands over her head again. They were going to cut off part of her ear! They'd send it to Courtney with a demand for money. How he was supposed to recognize it as hers, she'd never know. Weren't all ears alike, and was that what had happened to these thugs' ears? No, no one would hold them for ransom, she was certain. She was also certain she was on the verge of hysteria and didn't care. She was entitled.

"What's got her so riled, Ursie?" Quigley sounded worried.

Ursula shrugged. What did she know about pampered pets of the fancy? "Don't get yourself in a fidge, ducks. We're only going to cut off a curl or two to send him. He can put it in his watchcase after. A keepsake, don't you know?"

A lock of hair? Kathlyn started breathing again.

"Can I have one, too?" Sean begged, putting out his hand. "I never saw anything so pretty."

Quigley slapped him. "She's a lady, she is. Not for the likes of you."

So they took Kathlyn's curl—and her basket of food—and locked the door. Huddling in her cloak, for there was no heat, Kathlyn looked around. Her captors had left her in a tiny room with no window for climbing out of and no weapons for defending herself. It held one candle, one bed, and only one door, the one that the kidnappers had just gone through. Kathlyn could hear at least two of them speaking on the other side, so even if she could unlock her narrow cell with one of her hairpins, there was no escaping.

Kathlyn decided she had two choices: she could cry, which would avail her nothing, or she could wait patiently for his lordship to come to her rescue. Courtney would come, she knew he would, even if he didn't love her. He'd come out of his sense of responsibility, or sheer male pride in protecting what he'd claimed. Either that or else he'd pay the footpads' demands.

She'd make it up to him, Kathlyn swore. She would even marry him if he still wanted a female who was always falling into scrapes.

Emptying her cloak pockets in search of a peppermint candy or one of the molasses drops she carried for the children, Kathlyn discovered her book of sonnets. Very well, she told herself, she'd sit and read until the candle burned out. She'd pretend she was sitting on the ground at a picnic in Richmond, not on a hard bed in a glorified closet. She'd pretend it was summer, she was warm, and this was all a memory. She'd pretend those were only ants crawling up her legs.

Chapter Twenty-three

"What, have you been out in the sun too long?"

Inspector Dimm looked through the heavy damask drapes to get a glimpse of the sky. Last time he looked, that sun had been as dim as his name. Like the smallest dab of melted butter, it couldn't have covered one biteful of Mrs. Dawson's scones, much less fried his brain. "No, ma'am," he answered, "I thought that's what you meant about my finding your missing relation, Miss Kathlyn Partland."

"Don't even say that name!" Lady Bellamy held the sal volatile to her nose. "As for bringing her here this afternoon, I should say not! Why, the neighbors might see that wanton coming in my door. Worse, my daughters might meet her in the hall. Then we'd all be ditched. Their vouchers to Almack's, their presentations at court, invitations to balls—everything would be canceled if word got out that they'd associated with a fallen woman. And such a one!" That required another restorative inhale. "If anyone knew she was their cousin, they'd be tarred with the same brush, you may be assured. Bellamy'd be certain to hear of it, too, were she in this house. No, no, that is utterly past contemplating. How could you think such a thing?"

Mr. Dimm hadn't thought for one minute that Lady Bellamy wanted anything but to be reunited with her lost lamb. Then again, he hadn't thought she'd keep him standing in this parlor while she suffered a paroxysm of nerves. His feet were hurting already. Shifting his weight from side to side, the Runner asked, "Then what was it you had in mind, ma'am? Why were you sending to Bow Street to hire me?"

"To find the chit, of course, and get rid of her!"

Get rid of her? Dimm was liking this assignment less and less, to say nothing of the lady in her vast lace cap, with her chest draped in rows of pearls like a jeweler's case, or her beribboned lapdog gnarring near his ankles. "You wouldn't be thinking I'd be party to seeing an innocent subject carted off to gaol on some false charge, would you?" He was almost looking forward to threatening this ungracious, overbearing female with arrest for suborning one of His Majesty's officers.

Lady Bellamy sniffed at her salts again. "Of course not, that would only create more publicity. Aren't you listening? I want you to find the jade and convince her to leave London, no, England."

Dimm removed his spectacles to wipe them, while he wiped his hopes of any remuneration. "Finding Miss Partland is no problem, ma'am, but getting her to leave Town might be."

"Humph. Not with what I'm prepared to pay, sirrah, unless the gel is a total moron, besides a trollop. That's what I'm hiring you for, to make the bargain and make the arrangements. You'll get your reward when I know that . . . that hell-born bawd is on a boat somewhere."

Dimm eyed the nearest chair, then he eyed the decorated dust-ball snarling at him. He stayed put. "His lordship might have something to say about that."

Lady Bellamy snorted again. "Lord Chase? Faugh, he'll find another mistress as soon as there's a new cast of opera dancers." Bellamy always did. "And if rumors are to be believed, he already has another demirep in keeping."

"Well, there's rumors and there's rumors."

She brushed that aside. "I never believed that old bibble-babble. Fine figure of a man, the viscount is, despite the limp. Makes those gabble-grinders look no-account with this latest brouhaha. Two mistresses indeed." Not even Bellamy was so profligate; he'd likely have heart failure if he tried. "No matter, Chase will be glad to be spared the expense of this second bit of fluff. Costly creatures, kept women." Bellamy's must be, the way he always cried poverty when his wife wanted a new gown.

"I don't figure that's how his lordship's looking at it." Or liking his Miss Kitty mentioned in the same breath as chorus girls and courtesans.

Lady Bellamy wasn't listening. "Oh, my sister was such a willful chit. See what comes of not listening to those who know best? Papa found her a perfectly acceptable baron's son, but no, she had to have Partland. Bad blood will out, I say. Not that there was anything wrong with his family. I'm not a snob, of course."

"Of course," Dimm muttered.

"They were poor, however, poor and undistinguished. Not nearly a proper match for one of Lord Fowler's daughters. You can rest assured that my girls won't have the opportunity to make such a misalliance. I'll see they don't even meet any undesirables, once this little contretemps is cleared up."

Chancing the dog and the grande dame's displeasure, Dimm sat down. "Begging your pardon, ma'am, but mayhap there's another way of looking at the situation, one that won't be so costly either."

Her ears pricked up at that, he noted. So did the dog's. "Yes?"

"Well, 'pears to me your own gals' chances might improve, having a viscountess for a cousin."

"How droll." She tittered. "My good man, the chances

are better of your finding my diamonds than of Courtney Choate, Viscount Chase and heir to His Grace, the Duke of Caswell, marrying my niece. Perhaps you are unaware, but men of his caliber do not wed their mistresses."

Dimm was aware of that rug-rat showing its teeth. "That's right, they don't, not in the ordinary course of things, anyways. But his lordship don't seem to be your ordinary sort. Now, I'm likely wasting my breath, but I don't think Miss Partland is his mistress." He held up a hand to stop her objections. "I know it looks like she's his light-o'-love, like he meant it to seem. He's playing some deep game, what can only work in your favor, iffen you play your cards right. Believe what you will, but the fact is that the same gentleman what won't introduce his bit o' muslin to his mother, well, he won't ruin a good girl's reputation without making it right, neither."

"What are you saying, that my niece was an innocent until Lord Chase compromised her past redemption?"

"Not past redemption, ma'am, for seems to me the quickest way to restore a black rep is with a gold ring."

The smelling salts hit the floor, where the dog took one whiff and ran yipping from the room. "You actually think he'll marry her?"

Dimm actually thought Lord Chase was the worst bobbing-block to put on breeches, but he said, "I really think he's an honorable bloke. If he sees she's from a good family what's ready to help her regain her place with the Quality, then his sense of duty won't let him do anything else."

"He was an officer," Lady Bellamy reflected. "A hero."

"And he's rich as Croesus."

That convinced her. "I'll consider your suggestion, Mr. Dimm, once I've seen for myself if she's at all acceptable. I won't try to foist soiled goods off on society, for it cannot be done."

'Twere done all the time, from what Dimm gathered of the polite world, but he'd won his point, and a cup of tea while waiting for her ladyship to change for a visit to Mrs. Dawson's. Lady Bellamy still wasn't taking any chances with having her wayward niece brought here to Belgrave Square. She wasn't taking her crested carriage into that middle-class neighborhood either. And, she made it plain, she wasn't paying the investigator a single shilling until she smelled the orange blossoms in the church.

The rabbit fur lining her cloak was nice; the silver lining in this cloud of calamity was nice; the underlining in Kathlyn's book of sonnets was nicest yet. In that bare little room, with only a thin door and an ambitious extortion scheme separating her from cutpurses, killers, and kidnappers, Miss Partland finally figured out who had marked her book.

Poor Mr. Miner must have known he'd never make it back to Cheshire to retrieve the pilfered jewels, for he'd underlined the last words of the line "No longer mourn for me when I am dead." He then decided to reward the only person who was kind to him, marking the thirtieth sonnet: "For thy sweet love remember'd such wealth brings."

He knew Kathlyn would never keep stolen property, hence his hint about a reward coming her way, and he must have suspected her possessions would be searched, therefore using the faintest of markings while she and the other passengers were at supper in the inn, or that longer time when everyone but Mr. Miner left the coach to help free it from the snowbank.

At first it appeared he also feared she was dull-witted, for he underlined all three "summers" in "Shall I compare thee to a summer's day." But Kathlyn was from Cheshire, she knew the crossroads that divided Upper, Lower, and Old Summerfield. Kathlyn flipped through the pages, searching. "Forty winters," "lofty trees I see barren of leaves," "the little Love-god lying once asleep." All of the information must be there, but in no particular order, as Mr. Miner flipped through the pages. Forty paces from the signpost? Forty meters facing the trees? She couldn't find the way to the statue of Cupid! Oh, if only she had a pen and paper, she could figure it out!

Then Kathlyn remembered where she was. Oh dear. Perhaps it was a good thing she didn't have a pencil after all. Starting at the slender volume's beginning again, she tried memorizing each of the underlined clues, but she was too excited, and it really would be much easier if she were right there, finding the landmarks. Maybe his lordship would take her, she daydreamed instead. She'd give him half the reward money to repay him for her gowns and such. Why, she'd be freezing to death right now if not for the mantle he'd insisted she purchase. Then again, she wouldn't be here at all if not for his money. Once more reminded of her current predicament, Kathlyn decided to give the viscount the entire reward, for paying her ransom.

Of course, if he didn't come, she'd have to use the book and its messages as a negotiating chip for her freedom, which was not an appealing thought. Her new acquaintances did not appear the sort to be trusted to uphold their share of any bargain. Most crucial of all, she decided, was keeping her information and excitement hidden from the gang members. She turned back to the sonnets, the unmarked sonnets.

In faith, I do not love thee with mine eyes,
For they in thee a thousand errors note;
But 'tis my heart that loves what they despise,
Who, in despite of view, is pleas'd to dote.

Well, he was toplofty and arrogant, but Kathlyn couldn't think of a thing she'd change in the viscount, much less despise. The pride was part and parcel of who he was, what he was. As for her eyes, or her memory,

Kathlyn couldn't recollect a single defect. Master Shakespeare's poor ladylove must have been an antidote.

Your love and pity doth the impression fill
Which vulgar scandal stamp'd upon my brow;
For what care I who calls me well or ill,
So you o'er-green my bad, my good allow?

How true, that Kathlyn did not care nearly so much about the gossip and her loss of reputation now that Courtney seemed fonder of her.

You are my all-the-world. . . .

Ah, no wonder the Bard lived on, when he spoke such truth. Nothing mattered, not pride nor possessions, nothing except Courtney's love. And getting out of here.

Ursula brought her supper, a chicken leg and half a raspberry tart from the picnic basket, and agreed to bring her another candle. "Why not? We'll have the ready for a whole chandelier soon, all crystal prisms and gold chain. So what's that you're reading, ducks?"

It was all Kathlyn could do not to jump up and stuff the book under the mattress. Instead she held it out so Ursula could see the tooled cover. "Shakespeare's sonnets. Do you know them?"

"No, but my Harry did."

He certainly did. "A big reader, was he?"

"No, but he started out as an actor. He could recite whole scenes. Never made much sense, but he could spout them off like a regular jaw-me-dead."

"Would you like me to read aloud?" Kathlyn didn't want the other woman getting any ideas about borrowing the book. She needn't have worried.

"Too dry for me, ducks. I like a good farce now and again, and that's the extent of it."

She turned to leave, but Kathlyn asked, "Did you, ah, send the note to Lord Chase?"

"All right and tight. Sean's finding a boy to deliver it to that Choate House right now. You'll be out of here before the cat can lick its ear."

"But we were going to Richmond today. He may already have left."

Ursula shrugged. "We was going to send it to your love nest in Kensington, but that Runner chap is always hanging around."

"It's not my—" Then Kathlyn remembered Mr. Dimm. He'd keep Courtney from doing anything rash, thank goodness.

"It's not much of a place, now that I come to think on it. He could do a lot better by you, ducks. In fact, let me give you some advice for when this is over, 'cause I've been there. Start hinting for some jewelry. I noticed you didn't sport any at the Argyle Rooms, nor at Epsom, and now neither." Ursula didn't seem to admire Kathlyn's mulberry merino gown either, with its filled-in neckline. "Your gent might be a nip-farthing, but if you ask now while he's a-panting after you, he'll come through. And make sure he doesn't try to turn you up sweet with any trumpery beads. Diamonds is what you want. They're better'n money in the bank. You listen to me, a girl has to look out for her future."

"Ah, thank you. I'll try to remember. And speaking of the future, what if his lordship proves to be miserly indeed and refuses to ransom a mere acquaint—mistress? I mean, we haven't known each other very long, and he is a high stickler."

Ursula hunched her shoulders again, lowering her neckline by another indecent inch or two. "Well, we've got to get some cash for our efforts, ducks. I suppose we'll have to sell you to a brothel."

Chapter Twenty-four

"May the sun shine on you, good sir," the flower girl said when Courtney bought her last four bouquets of violets.

"Oh, it is, sweetheart, it is." Clouds were pushing across the sky, the temperature was hovering just above freezing—but they'd have their picnic. Yes, the sun was shining on the viscount today.

He was going to put his luck to the test again this afternoon, out in the country, out of the public eye. Kathlyn was a country girl, after all. He'd show her he enjoyed the simple pleasures in life, too. This time she'd accept, he just knew it. Courtney could feel it in her smiles, in the tremble of her hand lingering in his when he helped her out of the carriage yesterday. His plan was working: she was coming to like him.

He didn't think he was rushing his fences; he didn't think he could wait another day, not with Meg up and about. His precious ninny was liable to take the notion that she was unnecessary, that she should move out of Nanny's again. Unnecessary? Hah! Lord Chase meant to see that the only place she moved to was into his house.

Laughing at himself for behaving like a child who

couldn't wait for Christmas, Courtney counted the hours until he could fetch Kathlyn, drive to Richmond, and lose Meg's children in the maze. He'd have to bribe young Philip to stay lost an extra half hour. Just a few hours more, he told himself, right after he saw his man of affairs, who should have had time enough now to arrange the purchase of a special license.

First the viscount found a boy to carry one of the posies back to Choate House, with instructions to see it delivered to his mother. Courtney felt guilty about not discussing his plans with her, but she'd been so ill since her trip from Bath, keeping to her rooms, that he hadn't wanted to disturb her. Better he present her with a fait accompli anyway. She'd love Kathlyn, how could she not?

His mother would be devastated that there would be no huge wedding at St. George's, but Courtney wasn't waiting, not for gowns and guest lists. He'd waited his whole life. Every extra day was torture.

As soon as he had that special license in his hands, and Kathlyn's acceptance, they'd be wed. Perhaps as early as tomorrow, he decided, definitely before another sennight had passed. Hell, another sennight would likely see him frothing at the mouth. He only hoped Kathlyn wouldn't be as disappointed as his mother about having a small, private ceremony. He'd make it up to her, though, Courtney vowed, making sure her wedding bed was a bed of roses. No, rose petals. And he'd buy her the most beautiful wedding gown in creation, in about a year or two, when he got tired of looking at her body.

They'd honeymoon at his hunting box in Ireland, after a stop at Caswell Hall to introduce the new viscountess to the head of the family. His Grace would forgive the havey-cavey courtship, Courtney prayed, once he saw Kathlyn and the beautiful grandchildren she could give him. And if, by chance, Grandfather would not accept a tutor's daughter as the mother to his heirs, well, they'd just stay on in Ireland. What could be lovelier than Ireland in the spring, all blue sky and green grass? Courtney had a handsome income of his own and couldn't be disinherited from the succession or the entailments, but Lord Caswell's blessing would be gratifying, especially after all the nagging he'd done about Courtney getting legshackled.

The duke's approval would go a long way to seeing Kathlyn accepted in society, too. But if they didn't have that nod, if the new Lady Chase was not given vouchers to Almack's, well, Courtney was beyond caring about the tittle-tattle. He'd wasted too much of his own life trying to gain the polite world's respect. They could just stay in the country raising cows and carrots and blue-eyed cherubs. It would be London's loss, for no matter what anyone thought, Kathlyn was a lady. Kathlyn was *his* lady.

"A lady? Humph! I should like to see the day a lady bares her bosom at the Cyprians' Ball." Lady Bellamy had agreed to come to Kensington; she hadn't agreed to be agreeable. Inspector Dimm had introduced her to Mrs. Dawson, then wisely left to fetch Miss Partland back from Meg's.

"Seems to me I read in all the papers how ladies bare a lot more at those balls and such that last all night." Nanny sniffed at the bejeweled, beturbaned, and belittling matron who had condescended to sit on her chintz-covered sofa. "Dampened petticoats, no petticoats, muslin so thin you can see right through it. My girl was dressed respectably, compared to that."

"Your girl?" Lady Bellamy removed the lavender-scented handkerchief from under her nose long enough to ask.

Nanny forgave her that—she *was* sitting in Wolfie's usual place—but not the curled lip. "No one else seemed to claim her, did they? So Miss Kathlyn became part of my own family, such a love she is, and her with no kith nor kin to look after her, tsk, tsk."

Lady Bellamy felt the need to straighten the peacock feather in her turban, rather than reply, so Nanny went on: "Miss Kathlyn has been a treat to chaperone, too."

Now, that got Lady Bellamy's attention. "Chaperone?"

"What did you think, I don't know apes from apples?" Daggers couldn't have been sharper than Nanny's tone of voice. "I spent my life in gentlemen's homes. I know what's proper, I do, what's fitting for a Quality miss, even if she is down on her luck through no fault of her own. Almost every minute she's been here, she's been in my own company." Nanny chose to ignore the visit to the opera and that infamous ball, the times she herself was off at Meg's. Kathlyn and Courtney had never spent the night together, at any rate. "Other times she's been out in public or she's busy governessing my daughter's children."

"Governessing?"

"For your information, ma'am, your niece is an educator, a decent, honorable profession, just like her pa. She's been giving lessons to my Meg's boy and girl, who happen to be Lord Chase's godchildren." Nanny's eyes narrowed. "I hope you're not going to suggest that Miss Kathlyn could be aught but a lady with my grandchildren present? And you'd better not be accusing the boy that I helped raise of any fast behavior with a gentlewoman, either. Not in the house he provides for his old nursemaid, by heaven."

Lady Bellamy was still digesting: chaperone, governess, godchildren. Courtesan? It didn't go down easily. "Then you mean the chit's not . . . ?"

Nanny crossed her arms over her apron and scowled at the doyenne in her dog's seat. "There's no hanky-panky under my roof, never has been, never will be. And I won't give space on my sofa to anyone who says otherwise, fine feathers or not. Master Courtney is a gentleman to the core, the finest in the land, and Miss Kathlyn is a good girl. That anyone could think so poorly of their own blood relation should be a sin." Nanny *tsk*ed a few more times. "Of course, it's no more'n I'd expect from a 'lady' too proud to take in a tutor's daughter, and too cold-hearted to look after her own dead sister's orphan."

Lady Bellamy waved her lace-edged handkerchief. "That was merely a misfortunate misunderstanding. All in the past, don't you know. I mean to make it up to the dear girl now." By seeing her married to that wealthy, eligible libertine. "Do tell me about the viscount. Did I hear that he had two country properties or three?"

Lord Chase had his three remaining posies—for Nanny, Meg, and Kathlyn—and the special license, but he didn't have a ring. Blast! What kind of bounder asks a female to marry him without having a ring? The family heirlooms were in the vault at Caswell, except those in his mother's possession, which, being a dutiful son, Courtney did not relish wresting from his fond parent, especially when she was still so downpin from her journey. So he betook himself to Rundell and Bridge's.

The selection was immense, the quality was superb, the shop was a fishbowl. Half the matrons in Town seemed to be there this morning, and half their husbands, although not necessarily together nor purchasing baubles for each other. Almost no sales were made while the viscount, unaware, made his deliberations. So intent was Courtney on making the right choice, he didn't notice the traffic ebb and flow around him, with quizzing glasses and lorgnettes practically looking over his shoulder to see what he selected.

As soon as Courtney indicated his decision, a pear-shaped diamond surrounded by emeralds, hordes left the store, even before the viscount told the clerk to wrap the matching gold band. The elegantly understated ring wasn't gaudy enough for a bird of paradise, but it was too expensive for a casual toss or a relative. It cried "Engagement."

The men were off to change their bets at White's, the women were hurrying to add this dollop to the scandal-broth. And Lady Adelina Fostwick left the jewelry shop to throw herself off London Bridge.

Inspector Dimm did not find Miss Partland at Meg's. He found two disappointed children and one distressed mother. Meg wrapped up the baby and they all set out to look for Kathlyn and Ripken, who'd gone missing, too.

Another distressed mother was on her way to Nanny's. Lady Chase had tearfully concluded that staying in her room wasn't going to free her son from any profligate ways or any grasping harpies, so she decided to consult levelheaded Nanny Dawson. Actually, Lady Chase was hoping that Nanny might undertake the awkward task of talking some sense into the boy. He'd always listened to her better than his mother anyway. Clutching her sodden handkerchief and her bouquet of violets, the viscount's mother dragged herself out of her carriage and up the walk.

If Inspector Dimm were there, he'd be sure to say "Gorblimey." And where was that man, Nanny wanted to know, leaving her with two grande dames in diamonds, in high dudgeon? They were eyeing each other like stray cats in the alley, fur up, backs arched.

"We are acquainted, Nanny." Lady Chase saved Mrs. Dawson from making the introduction, bowing her head the merest fraction in the other woman's direction as a sop to courtesy. "Although I cannot imagine what brings you here, Madorra. I thought you'd be home counting your husband's money." So much for courtesy.

"And I'm surprised to see you away from your quacks in Bath, Rosemary. But I'm here, of course, to see justice done for my poor innocent niece, led astray by an evil seducer."

Lady Chase turned to Nanny, who was wringing her apron. "Didn't you lend me a novel with that plot last month? Really, Madorra, whatever your business, I wish you'd leave. I have to speak to Mrs. Dawson. In private."

"I'm not leaving without my niece, and not without an honest offer of marriage for her."

"From Nanny? Who in the world is your niece, anyway? I heard you were bringing your fubsy-faced chits out this year, but nothing about a niece."

"Fubsy-faced? Fubsy-faced?" Lady Bellamy sputtered. "Why, you . . . you . . . bounder-begetter. My niece is Kathlyn Partland, whom your son has ruined!"

"Good grief, he cannot have *another* woman!" The viscountess fell back in her chair, clutching her handkerchief to her heart. "What did we do wrong, Nanny?"

"Humph! Mealymouthed as ever, I see. Kathlyn Partland, my only sister's girl, has been traduced by your son into pretending to be his mistress, one Kitty Parke."

"Kitty Parke is your niece? And you dare to advertise it? You have as much gall as ever, I see. Well, you can find your niece and take her away with my blessings. I'm sure the world will be a better place with one less fallen woman."

Lady Bellamy raised her chins. "My niece is an innocent, and you can ask your own Mrs. Dawson. She, at least, agrees that your son should do the decent thing by Kathlyn."

Lady Chase jumped to her feet and shook her fist in the other woman's face. "Oh, no, you don't, Madorra Fowler, you're not going to snabble a viscount for this sewer-bred slut of yours! It didn't work when you wanted *my* viscount, and it won't work now! I'll see you in hell before I see my son married to Kitty Parke!"

Lady Bellamy was on her feet now, too. "And I'll see him in court for breach of promise. And I never wanted your weak-chinned, womanizing weasel of a viscount, anyway, so there!"

"Why, you—"

"Mama, Mama, Miss Kitty's gone missing!" Meg rushed into the room and thrust the baby into Nanny's hands. "The children and I are going with Mr. Dimm to ask the neighbors if they've seen her or Mr. Ripken."

Lady Chase waved at Meg's departing back and smiled like the cat who swallowed the canary. "There, your innocent miss has run off with this Ripken person."

Lady Bellamy had a moment's doubt. Good grief, what if the gel had done a flit? What if she, Madorra Bellamy, had believed Dimm's Banbury tale about a wager and a lost position and a carefully chaperoned stay with an old nursemaid? She'd have given Kitty Parke's real name to her worst enemy, that's what. Then she remembered who Ripken was. *No* female, no matter how desperate or depraved, would run off with Ripken. "Oh, my stars, she's been arrested!" She grabbed for her vinaigrette.

Lady Chase started weeping again. "And you'll drag my son's name into whatever bumblebroth she's made, I know."

Nanny glared at both of them in disgust. "Most likely she's gone to check on Lizzie's mother, and Ripken went along to carry her basket, the nodcock. I'll go fetch them back before we have the militia out." Then Nanny remembered the infant in her arms. She looked at Lady Bellamy, then she looked at Lady Chase. She put the child on the sofa between them and turned to the dog. "You watch the baby, Wolfie."

Chapter Twenty-five

"Then let not winter's ragged hand deface In thee thy summer . . ." Kathlyn read on. She'd figured out all the clues, scanned through all the sonnets. The jewels were in the fourth tree to the right of the crossroads, marked by an arrow. Or else they were in a summerhouse under a clock case shaped like a Cupid. Or both. Now she was starting over, doing anything to keep her morbid thoughts at bay. ". . . Be not self-will'd, for thou art much too fair To be death's conquest and make worms thine heir." Ugh! She flipped through the pages until she found a favorite: "For nothing this wide universe I call, Save thou, my rose; in it thou art my all." Yes, he'd come.

Lord Chase drove directly to Meg's house to fetch his fellow picnickers. No one was there. He thought he must be all about in his head, head over heels, in fact, to forget their arrangements. They must all be waiting for him at Nanny's.

They weren't. His mother and a jewel-draped dragon in a turban were alone in the little parlor, nervously eyeing Meg's baby, who was asleep on the sofa.

Courtney bowed to his mother, who was still clutching her violets. The viscount had the other three bouquets in his gloved hand. "Come to visit Nanny, have you, Mother? Excellent. Perhaps she'll have a potion to cure your megrims."

"I have a potion for what ails you, you rakeshame!" the woman in the feathered turban snarled at him. "It's parson's—"

Courtney was about to take his looking glass out to give this encroaching female a setdown, even if she was a friend of his mama's, when that lady spoke up: "You needn't pay her any mind, Courtney, I never did. But if you are looking for your soiled dove, she has flown the coop." And she smiled in satisfaction, until she saw the thunderclouds on her son's brow. "Well, Nanny and Meg are out looking for her and some Ripken person, although I cannot imagine why."

"Blast! Kitty wouldn't have gone off without telling someone, and she wouldn't have disappointed the children either." To say nothing of him. Courtney paced the narrow room until, predictably, a solution presented itself. "I'll kill them this time, I swear I will."

He tossed the violets at Lady Bellamy with, "My compliments, ma'am," and left, slamming the door behind himself. Which woke up Baby, who started crying.

"You can't expect me to—"

"Well, I'm not going to—"

Woody and Algie were at White's, making their fortunes in the betting book, until Lord Chase strode into that hallowed chamber and hollered, "Where's Kitty and what have you two muckworms done with her this time?"

All bets were off. The wench had taken French leave. With Chase's flaming temper, who could blame her? First Marlowe's chit, then this new dasher. The older members shook their heads. Algie and Woody shook in their boots, until they managed to convince the viscount that they'd been at White's all morning. They hadn't abducted Miss Kitty, hadn't seen Miss Kitty, and wouldn't harm a hair on Miss Kitty's beautiful head if they did happen to trip over her.

"Well, someone did."

Pity that someone. The viscount stopped off at Choate House for his dueling pistols, Algie and Woody hard on his heels as soon as they'd placed their new wagers. Their money was still on the viscount. If he didn't find Kitty, they'd be up River Tick. They offered to help.

Chase's butler tried to hand him a soiled twist of paper that had lately been delivered by a street-urchin messenger.

"Not now, Henniker. Can't you see I'm in a hurry?"

When he returned to Kensington, Courtney found his mother cooing over Meg's baby, while the other dowager was dangling her necklace in front of him. The infant appeared to be sucking on a pearl the size of a sparrow's egg. There was no news.

Then Meg came to collect the baby. She'd take the children and wait at home, in case there was word there. Nanny returned, shaking her head. Lizzie hadn't seen hide nor hair of Miss Kitty. Now Nanny had two strange bucks of the first stare in her little parlor, besides two highborn she-bears. Heavens, King George was liable to stop by next. Well, she knew how to manage the young gentlemen. Nanny went to fix sandwiches and slice cake.

Before she'd gone far, Mr. Dimm set up a shouting in the street, so they all rushed to see. The Runner was hurrying along behind Little George, who was carrying an unconscious Ripken. They'd found him, Mr. Dimm explained once he'd caught his breath and had a restorative sip of his lordship's cognac, stashed behind some crates in an alley. His clothes were disordered, he had a huge knot on the back of his head, a red wig clutched in his hand, and a smile on his face.

"Damn, he can't tell us anything," the viscount cursed, after Nanny tried to rouse the fallen Runner with Lady Bellamy's vinaigrette. She was eyeing the feathers on that lady's turban, for burning, when Little George tapped her shoulder. He kept pointing to his own chest and nodding.

"Yes, yes, George, you found him. Good boy." She smiled as best she could and nodded back. Little George was pounding his chest now and bobbing his head up and down.

"Wait, maybe he knows something." The viscount tugged on George's sleeve to get his attention. Trying to speak slowly, in case Little George could understand his lip movements, Courtney asked, "Did you see what happened?" Little George put his hands over his ears. "Yes, I know you're deaf! Blast, where's his slate, Nanny?"

"He must have lost it outside. And look, he's all tuckered out. Not from carrying that featherweight, I'd guess."

With Little George still holding his head, Courtney shouted for a pad and pencil. Algie handed a page over, with his figuring of the current odds on the back. Courtney drew a cat and a big question mark. "Miss Kitty?"

Little George looked at the drawing, shook his head, and brought him Wolfie.

Courtney added whiskers. George grabbed the pad and drew his stick figure of two men, one tall, one short, and both with one ear.

"Gorblimey, I was right!" Inspector Dimm was looking over the viscount's shoulder. "It's the Diamond Miner Gang! Quigley had an ear sliced off in gaol once."

Lady Bellamy snatched her vinaigrette back from Nanny. "What, the ones who stole my diamonds?"

Courtney turned to look. "I was wondering who the devil you were. You're the aunt who let Kathlyn come to London with no resources, who wouldn't give her shelter? Your own niece?"

Algie grabbed his paper back.

"Pish-tish," Lady Bellamy said, "I misplaced her direction, is all. And I came here to rescue the dear girl as soon as I heard she was in London, where, I might say, you've managed to make a mull of things."

"My son never led a female astray in his life, you old—"

"He lost her, didn't he?"

Courtney was nearly tearing his hair out. "I'll find her, by all that's holy. But where, blast it?" He didn't even know where to start searching.

Mr. Dimm was still holding that red wig. "Methinks I might have a glimmer on't. I met a widow lady in the park a while back. Seemed particularly interested in my line of work, she did. After a bit, I escorted her home to her place in Chelsea. Didn't go up, don't you know," he added for Nanny's benefit. "Thing is, I made the jarvey bide a few houses down so I could see the female safe in her door. Gentlemanly thing to do, don't you know?"

"Hell and damnation, man, what's this got to do with Miss Partland?" the viscount demanded. "So you're a regular Romeo in a red vest. Where's Kathlyn?"

"I'm getting to that, if you'll hold your fire." Mr. Dimm studied the wig, a little longer than necessary. "You see, the widow—she had a veil on, and dark hair— never went in the door she pointed to."

Courtney was listening more intently, as was the rest of the Runner's audience except for Ripken, who was still unconscious on the sofa, and Little George, of course.

"No, she went clean past that house and down the block to another one altogether. Suspicious, I'd say."

Algie nudged Woody. "I'd say she didn't want any old coot calling on her the next day."

Everyone ignored him, waiting for Mr. Dimm's next words. "The way I sees it, the female is Harry Miner's widow, what has bright yellow hair. She must be here a-looking for the jewels, too. I'd lay odds that's where them villains have taken Miss Partland, to Ursula Miner's flat."

"What odds?" Algie asked, but no one answered.

Courtney was pulling on his gloves. "Deuce take it, Kathlyn doesn't have the blasted jewels!"

"Then we'd best get over there in a hurry, Cap'n, wouldn't you say?"

"Go on and fetch Missy home," Nanny called after them, "and you take care now," without specifying which rescuer had her concern.

Lady Bellamy was not so ambiguous. "You bring my niece back here, Chase, or I'll . . . I'll . . ."

"What, try to make him marry one of your fubsy-faced daughters? Be careful, dear," the viscountess told her son, magnanimously refraining from expressing her hopes that the Miner Gang had set sail to China, with Madorra Fowler's niece in tow.

Courtney was out the door. "I'll keep searching till I find her, as if my very life depended on it. It does."

Lady Chase sighed and dabbed at her eyes. "He does seem to care for her."

Lady Bellamy snorted. "Humph, anyone can see he's top over trees for her. That man Dimm just might be right: Chase means to marry the chit."

Nodding sadly, the viscountess asked, "And you say the father was a tutor?"

"Respectable enough, though undistinguished. I daresay it will do. With my connections I can see she's not ostracized, once they're married, of course."

Lady Chase sat up. "Well, I'm sure I have enough social influence to see she's accepted everywhere."

"Pish-tish. She's Lord Fowler's granddaughter. I daresay I ought to be able to bring her into fashion if she's the Diamond they're calling her."

"Fustian, she'll be married to Lord Caswell's heir. I'm sure I can have her declared a Toast, if she's as prettily behaved as Nanny says."

"Well, I won't have you planning any hole-in-corner marriage ceremony, as if there's something to be ashamed of in my niece's breeding or character."

"And I won't permit you to throw another of your nip-farthing affairs for the wedding breakfast."

"Why, you—"

"You old—"

Chapter Twenty-six

"Come sundown you'll be out of here, ducks." Ursula unlocked Kathlyn's cubby and offered her five grapes from the picnic basket. "Sean says he watched the boy deliver our note to your viscount's house."

By sundown Kathlyn would be frozen, starving, and petrified, if she hadn't itched herself to pieces by then.

Ursula spit grape seeds onto the floor near Kathlyn's bed. "Sean's mad we didn't ask for more blunt from your man. Says the swell can afford it, judging by the place. A regular palace, it is, with columns and marble steps. You ever seen it?"

Kathlyn shook her head, no.

"That's the way of it with the gentry, so don't be disappointed you ain't invited to tea."

Kathlyn allowed as how she wouldn't fret over the lapse.

"And rich folks—" another seed sent into the corner "—they don't share. That's how they stay rich." Ursula fingered Kathlyn's beloved blue pelisse. "Next time hold out for ermine, ducks. He can pay the dibs, and rabbit is for amateurs."

"Did you say the viscount would be coming for me at

sundown?" Kathlyn asked while Ursula seemed in a talkative mood.

"Oh, he don't come here, ducks. We're not dicked in the nob, you know, telling him where to find us. Might as well make the trade at Newgate. No, Sean and me go to meet your boyfriend at Shippy's at five. That's down by the docks where there's lots of traffic, not much in the way of law enforcement, you might say. We meet, we get the blunt, and lover-boy gets the address of Mother McCrory's, where Quigley'll be taking you as soon as we send word back."

Kathlyn very much feared that Lord Chase already knew the address of Mother McCrory's, for it was the brothel he'd driven her to on her first night in London. Kathlyn also had enough experience of the demimonde by now to realize that his lordship would also know half the gentlemen there. It wouldn't matter if he was recognized, but Courtney could never again profess her a lady if she was seen leaving such an establishment, not without becoming a laughingstock among his friends. Kathlyn would be an embarrassment, branded a scarlet woman for the rest of her life. Her lonely, lonely life.

When Ursula left, Kathlyn went back to her latest pastime, composing sonnets in her head rather than rereading them.

If thou love'st me, thou wouldst come,
Hours ago, and not leave me glum.

Some time later, after Kathlyn had composed at least a dozen paeans in praise of Lord Chase's noble spirit, and an equal number of poems pertaining to his tardiness, she heard her captors arguing in the other room. Quigley wanted to go along with the others to Shippy's, it seemed.

"You and Sean'll split the take without me, hop on a boat, and be sailin' off afore I deliver the wench."

"You're wrong," Ursula told him, fully intending to

bash Sean over the head and keep *all* of the ransom money. "And we already agreed we can't leave Kitty here by herself with Sean, 'cause he's liable to cut off all her hair or something worse, then where'd we be?"

"I could go alone," Sean offered, too eagerly. Both of the others slapped the smaller man.

Quigley scratched his head, then his crotch. This was a real dilemma. "I s'pose we could all go, 'n make sure the money gets divvied right."

Kathlyn held her breath—and a hairpin, for breaking out once they were gone—but no such luck. Ursula argued, "But then we don't get any blunt for the girl, in case his lordship turns into a Captain Sharp."

"Then why don't we take the mort with us? We can dump her out on a dock if he comes across with the rhino."

Kathlyn waited, but no one suggested what they would do with her down by the docks if the viscount decided she wasn't worth the bother.

> *How I pray'st thou won't be cheap,*
> *Lest they tosseth me in the deep.*

They had the place surrounded. A mouse couldn't have slipped through the net. A cockroach, perhaps, but not a mouse. Courtney would have charged inside if he'd had his way, both pistols primed and loaded, but Inspector Dimm was more cautious.

"I'd like to live long enough for my next retirement, I would," he chided the other's impatience. " 'Sides, you don't want us taking any chances with Miss Kathlyn's safety, do you?"

So they waited for reinforcements: the Watch, the constabulary, five more Runners, and a cousin by marriage of Mr. Dimm's who was handy with his fives. There were men at the front door, men at the back, guards on the rooftop and along the alleyways, in case any of the maggots tried to jump out a window. Algie and Woody took up positions across the street, protecting the carriage against a quick getaway. Mr. Dimm spit on the curb. "Gormless civilians."

Then they were ready. Dimm gave the order, and he, the viscount, and two others moved as quietly as they could to the third-story flat. "I hereby order you to open in the name of the law!" he shouted, but Courtney wasn't waiting. He kicked at the door with his good leg, then smashed the lock with his fist and burst inside.

"Oh, it's you."

Kathlyn was kneeling over three bloody bodies, trying to stop all of them from bleeding to death at once, it looked like. Courtney had seen whole engagements on the Peninsula with less gore. Kathlyn pointed to the female. "I hit Ursula with the fireplace poker while she was aiming her pistol at Sean. She shot him anyway. Of course, Sean had just stabbed Quigley, so I suppose he deserved it. I don't think any of them will die, do you?"

Courtney raised her to her feet, letting Dimm and his minions take over preserving the Miner Gang until their trial. "Hell and damnation, woman, you are as white as a ghost and covered in blood, and you're worried about the kidnappers? Deuce take it, I'm ready to bash the bastards with the poker myself for what they've done. I've been beside myself with worry, what with waiting for Dimm and his men to get in place . . . and what the bloody hell do you mean, 'Oh, it's you'?"

He reached up to brush a fallen lock of hair away from her face. "Are you all right, my dear?"

Kathlyn took one look at his hand, the hand that he'd used to break the lock, said, "Oh heavens, you're bleeding," and fainted dead away in Courtney's arms.

Well, that was more like it, Courtney thought. At least he could feel the littlest bit heroic, carrying his intrepid love to the carriage. The dratted stubborn damsel had gone and rescued herself! Not that he would have wished the darling girl harmed, of course, he just missed the added bit of luster on his armor.

210

That luster was in her eyes, though, when she woke up in the carriage in his arms, in his lap. She smiled at him and wrapped her arms more firmly around his neck and shoulder. Courtney brushed a kiss on her forehead, telling her, "If you say, 'Oh, it's you,' I'll toss you right out of the carriage."

Kathlyn grinned. "I knew you'd come."

"Of course I'd come. You never doubted that, did you? I'm only sorry I wasn't faster, sorry I couldn't protect you from the whole experience. But it will never happen again, my dear."

"Of course not, the gang will go to gaol."

"No, it will never happen again, my precious, because I'll never let you out of my sight again. I'll never let you near another fireplace poker, either." And then he kissed her, not like a chaste knight saluting his lady, not like a lord relieved that his property was unscathed, and not like an inexperienced, bumbling schoolboy. He kissed her like a lover, binding his soul to hers, and she kissed him back, all the way home to Kensington.

Lady Bellamy took one look at her niece, all rumpled and mussed, hair every which way, and covered with welts, and decided that a small wedding might be best after all. Small and soon, she amended, noting the besotted look on the chit's face.

Lady Chase saw her son carrying in a bloodstained baggage and fainted dead away in her chair.

The viscount tenderly placed Kathlyn on the sofa, Ripken having been sent home in a hackney, and Wolfie having resignedly claimed a space on the hearthside rug.

"Mr. Dimm's on his way," Courtney told Nanny, who was torn between trying to revive her former employer, trying to wipe the blood off Kathlyn, and trying to look out the window. The viscount took the towel and basin from his old nursemaid, to do the job on his beloved himself. "He'll be here as soon as he makes his report, but he's fine. And Algie and Woody went to their clubs, so you don't have to worry about them showing up looking to be fed. Only our Kathlyn here, whose worst misfortune seems to have been missing the picnic lunch."

Kathlyn was restored with a hearty tea, Lady Chase with a hearty swig of brandy. "My son is a hero," she told the room at large.

Laughing, Courtney said, "The lady saved herself." He was still sitting on the sofa, holding Kathlyn's hand.

She smiled back at him. "Oh, but you would have."

Lady Bellamy cleared her throat. "Enough of this April and May folderol. We have a wedding to plan." She and Lady Chase started to describe the nuptials they'd devised. Courtney was willing to let them natter on; he'd get Kathlyn aside later and convince her that the special license would burn a hole in his pocket if not used in a fortnight. A sennight, considering that kiss.

But Kathlyn wasn't paying attention. "I will not have his lordship forced into marrying me by circumstances beyond his control."

Tut-tutting, her aunt advised her to listen to wiser heads. "You don't want to follow in your mother's footsteps, child. See where it got her? An early grave, a daughter unprovided for."

"My mother loved my papa!"

"Pish-tish, what's that to the point? You've gone so far beyond the pale that nothing can save you except marriage, and no other man would ever have you. Without a ring on your finger, I cannot even invite you into my home. Such a blemished reputation would reflect badly on your cousins, don't you know. No, you'll have to marry him."

Lady Chase made an unladylike noise. "Let the girl be, Madorra. If she doesn't want to marry Courtney, she doesn't have to. I can find her a position with those relations of mine in Edinburgh."

"No!" shouted Lady Bellamy, seeing dreams of her daughters being launched at Choate House, at the viscount's expense, vanishing in air. "Her reputation will always be tarnished."

And "No!" shouted Lord Chase. "I won't let her go."

Quietly interjecting a polite cough, Kathlyn said, "Pardon me for interrupting your plans for my future, but I have a suggestion. It seems to me that an engagement ring will work as well as a wedding band. In fact, a hurried wedding will give rise to even more rumors. But if we give out that we're betrothed, and have had a secret engagement for ages, the ton might forgive our bending the rules."

"Bending the rules, hah! You broke every one of them, missy, but it just might work." And it just might give Lady Bellamy time to convince the peagoose where her best interests lay.

Kathlyn turned to the viscount. "You see? We could have a proper engagement for a month or two, after which my name will be cleared and your honor will be satisfied."

Courtney was on his feet, pacing, almost tripping over the feet of the older ladies in the narrow room. Wolfie gave up and padded out to the kitchen. "Thunderation, no! What, I should have another broken engagement in my dish? Not on your life! Another 'we have decided we don't suit'? Like hell we don't. We suit to a cow's thumb. And if you're hoping to find another eligible *parti*, someone you'll like better, no honorable man will approach you whilst we're engaged, so you can give up that idea."

Kathlyn knew she'd never find any man she could like better, but she'd have him of his own free will or not at all. "Then I'll go start my school, or take that post your mother mentioned."

"What, you'd be a drudge in some barren Highland fortress rather than marry me?"

"Rather than marry an unwilling husband, yes. You do not wish to marry me, my lord."

Courtney pounded the mantel with his sore hand, then

winced. "Miss Partland, how many times have I asked you to marry me?"

"Oh, three or four, I suppose, but they don't count. They were all about your honor and male pride and doing the proper thing to satisfy the conventions. You don't want *me*."

He picked up the discarded violets that had been sat on, stepped on, and never set in water. Thrusting them into her hand, Courtney sank to his knees beside her sofa. "Miss Kathlyn Partland, I cannot think of anything I have ever wanted more in my entire life than to marry you." He remembered he still had the ring in his pocket, so he pulled that out and pressed it into her hand, too. "I sincerely believe that I have but one heart, one love to give, and I have been waiting forever just to give it to you."

"But . . . but our lives have been so different. We have nothing in common."

"Do you love me?"

"Of course."

"Are you a virgin?"

Blushing, she replied, "You know I am!"

"There, that's two things in common right off. Nothing else matters, my love."

"Oh, Courtney," she said through tears of happiness, "you are my all-the-world."

He sat back. "I suppose that's better than 'Oh, it's you,' but what the deuce does it mean?"

"It means I've spent too much time with Master Shakespeare, that's all."

"Blasted bookishness! Does it mean yes?"

"Of course it does, my love."

Chapter Twenty-seven

The sun was shining on the wedding, of course. It wasn't the bright, clear sunshine of May or June that Lady Bellamy wished, but a soft yellow glow that kissed winter good-bye.

The little chapel was filled with roses and rare orchids from conservatories, and the first spring wildflowers from the countryside, snowdrops and myrtle. The Bellamy sisters were bridesmaids, and Meg's older children were ring bearer and flower girl. Mr. Dimm gave the bride away, Mrs. Dawson signed as witness, the dowager viscountess wept, and Lady Bellamy gloated that the Bellamy diamonds were finer than anything Lady Chase owned. Algie and Woody stood up with the groom, making book on the arrival of the first child and whether it would be the heir or not. The duke had decided not to attend; he'd save his energy for dandling his grandchildren on his knee, or that new barmaid at the local tavern. Instead, he sent the wedding couple a priceless statue of Astarte—a fertility goddess, what else?

And the bride and groom? Well, the love that glowed in their hearts would keep them warm for the rest of their lives, no matter the weather.

* * *

"A fine piece of detective work," Nanny Dawson congratulated Mr. Dimm after all the guests had left.

"What, seeing those two were a match? 'Twere as plain as the noses on them Bellamy girls."

Nanny dabbed at her eyes. "I knew Miss Kathlyn was a real lady, right from the start."

"Aye, and didn't she make that squeezecrab aunt pay out the reward money so she could share it with all her friends? That's Quality."

Nanny sniffed again. "I'll miss the dear girl. It was lovely having the young people around. It makes me wish I had more than the one chick."

"Do you now?" Mr. Dimm handed over his linen handkerchief. "Did I ever tell you about my son Gabriel or my girl Sarah? Then there's my sister's brood, and my cousin's boy who stays with me on school vacations. . . ."

A ray of sunshine woke Kathlyn on the morning after her wedding, that and the kisses her new husband was feathering across her eyelids. Courtney was smiling, dimples and all. "I told you I'd know how to do it."